To. Derrick + Jo
with lots of
love
Cyril ⊗
17/1/07

A Military Miscellany

A catalogue record of this book is available from the British Library

First Edition: December 2006

ISBN: 1-84375-276-X

To order additional copies of this book please visit:
http://www.upso.co.uk/charlesstacey

Published by: UPSO Ltd
5 Stirling Road, Castleham Business Park,
St Leonards-on-Sea, East Sussex TN38 9NW United Kingdom
Tel: 01424 853349 Fax: 0870 191 3991
Email: info@upso.co.uk Web: http://www.upso.co.uk

A Military Miscellany

by

Charles Stacey

MORE THAN AN APOLOGY

MORE THAN AN APOLOGY

In the midst of World War II, Douglas Stewart, a poet who was born in New Zealand but, since 1938, had lived in Australia, wrote the poem below - as one of his 'Sonnet to the Unknown Soldier':

WE DID NOT BURY HIM DEEP ENOUGH;
BREAK UP THE MONUMENT, OPEN THE TOMB,
STRIP OFF THE FLAGS AND THE FLOWERS
AND LET US LOOK AT HIM PLAINLY, NAKED MAN.
GREET HIM WITH SILENCE
SINCE ALL SPEECHES WERE LIES,
CLOTHE HIM IN FRESH KHAKI, HAND HIM A RIFLE
AND TURN HIM LOOSE TO
WANDER THE CITY STREETS
WHERE EYES SO QUICKLY INURED
TO DEATH'S ACCOUTREMENT
WILL HARDLY SPARE HIM A GLANCE,
EQUIPPED TO DIE FOR US,

YOU SEE THAT FELLOW WITH THE GRIN,
ONE EYE ON THE GIRLS,
THE OTHER ON THE PUB,
HIS UNIFORM SHABBY ALREADY?
WELL, DON'T LET HIM HEAR US,
BUT HE'S THE UNKNOWN SOLDIER,

THEY JUST LET HIM OUT,
THEY SAY HE LIVES FOR EVER.
THEY PUT HIM AWAY WITH FLOWERS AND FLAGS
AND FORGOT HIM,
BUT HE ALWAYS COMES WHEN THEY WANT HIM.
HE DOES THE FIGHTING.

On the morning of the 7th November 1920, Major Ronald Hughes, Royal Engineers, Officer-in-Charge of 79th Field Company, Royal Engineers, entered the adjoining office of his Company Sergeant Major Donald Miller in Belgium.

At his greeting 'Good morning, Sergeant Major' - Miller rose easily from behind his desk. 'Good morning, Sir', he replied.

'Had this order from Brigade Headquarters this morning asking us to provide four wooden stretchers. Nothing elaborate required -just plain wood - deal possibly. What have we got left of that timber the chaps felled recently in the Ancre area?' 'More than enough for the job', was the reply.

'Well, I'll leave it to you, and by the way, when finished the items are to be collected by members of the 45th Field Ambulance, RAMC, who are arranging their disposal to the units mentioned in the order. Just give them a call and they'll come over and collect.'

'Right, sir', Miller replied, glancing briefly at the order given to him.

When about to leave, the Major turned and said 'my wife and I had an invite to a social do at DIV HQ. It's tomorrow night and the maid's day off - I don't suppose there's a chance that you are free and could step in once again and help us out by being at our Quarters and keeping an eye on Nicholas, is there? Shouldn't be late back, say 11pm at the latest.'

Miller, who was awaiting the arrival on the station for his own wife and children, agreed at once... he had served as a Corporal in the war recently over, in the 174th Tunnelling Company, RE, when Major Hughes had been a 2nd Lieutenant, in the same unit. In the Fricourt area of the Somme in 1916, the unit had tunnelled to a depth of 80 feet in hard chalk beneath the German lines. It was dangerous, nerve-wracking underground warfare with the Germans counter-mining. Once, during a counter explosion, he had been trapped and it was Hughes who had dug through and rescued him. It was a close bond, that both, as Regular Soldiers, valued greatly.

He liked Nicholas, the four-year-old son. At his bedtime, the boy had always asked for 'one of your stories' before he went to sleep.

The usual routine went 'Many years ago across the sea, there lived a King who had a very handsome and brave son called...'
'Nicholas' was the boy's swift interjection.

Having settled the nomenclature, Miller would continue with the story suitably embellished with deeds of bravery and adventurous activities, until the soft breathing of the boy drifted him away to a dreamland of his own.

The Brigade Order referred to by Major Hughes, had been issued by Brigadier-General M Black, General Officer Commanding British Troops in France and Belgium, who was also Deputy Director of the War Graves Commission.

In early October 1920, he had been informed that the War Office had agreed to the proposal that a body of an unknown British Soldier would be recovered from each of the four main battle areas, the Somme, Arras, Aisne and Ypres and that the body eventually chosen was to be subsequently interred with all the dignity the State could provide in Westminster Abbey.

The initial suggestion that such a tribute should be paid to the grand total of 3,049,772 casualties in the war was made by a Regimental Padre of the East Surrey Regiment, to Dean B Sides of Westminster Abbey. The latter approached Field Marshall Sir William Graser, GCB, KCB, CB, DSO, MC and Bar at the War Office who considered it a sound suggestion but added a rider to the effect that the words 'unknown soldier' were limited to the military and that, possibly, the word 'warrior' be used to cover the Navy and Air Force. Dean Sides was then advised to contact the King on the latter's return from Balmoral.

When so apprised of the proposal, HM King George allegedly was none too keen on the idea but, on giving the matter serious thought, became greatly interested in the plan, going so far as to contribute one of his antique swords from his private collection at Windsor, to be affixed to the eventual coffin, as 'a soldier's gift to a soldier'. Actually, he was more of a Naval person for he liked boats and sailing.

Company Sergeant Major Miller duly contacted 45th Field Ambulance Unit RAMC, and four field ambulances, each containing an officer and two Other Ranks, the latter having shovels and sacks, arrived and a wooden stretcher was placed in each vehicle. The ambulances were then driven to their designated region being the battle areas mentioned in the Brigade Order. Not one of the four parties of Officers and Other Ranks were to be aware of the true reason for the work to be undertaken, that being to find an unknown British soldier's grave and exhume the body found there.

They were told also to make certain that the body exhumed was at a state of advanced decomposition. This instruction seemingly was that the Unknown Soldier gave off no putrid or noxious odour from decaying flesh in the hallowed precincts of Westminster Abbey. Of course, this may be merely hearsay, but it was stressed that there should be no need to cremate the remains of the dead soldier.

There were other provisions such as the choice of a body of a soldier killed in the early part of the war - possibly a Regular soldier of the original British Expeditionary Force - rather than a soldier of an equally catastrophic military disaster with appalling and tragic losses, for instance the inexcusable slaughter of the Somme battles of 1916 - men and boys, almost all civilian volunteers of Kitchener's New Army. Such nitpicking after such a conflict entailing so many casualties scarcely does justice to those who fought, died, were wounded physically, mentally in the Great War for Civilisation, or to those who survived the frightfully contested battle lines.

Whatever the views of senior army officers in their minuted discussion, their views were totally wrong and did no justice to themselves in their blinkered views or to the many grieving kith and kin of those servicemen who died subsequent to the 1914/15 battles.

However, the four parties, as instructed, confirmed from items of equipment, clothing, etc. on or in the immediate vicinity of the body, that it was that of a British soldier. Should any means of identification be found on the body, another corpse lacking such identification was to be found and exhumed. The chosen body was then covered in sacking, placed on the wooden stretcher and taken in the ambulance to Brigadier-General Black's General Headquarters, some forty kilometres west of Arras. Their arrival times were staggered and, once their task was completed, they returned immediately to their respective units, so that no possibility of a collusion regarding each task and location existed.

The Reverend William Dear at GHQ examined each corpse, determined it was a 'British Soldier' and could not be identified apart from that fact. The four bodies were then placed on their stretchers in a small hut that served as a chapel, each covered by a Union Jack.

It is from this point on that many accounts of what later took place in the hut in question, have been aired, and, indeed, published. One account is that once the stretchers had been placed side by side, all those concerned with the operation up until the moment retired to a distance and that an officer who had never been inside the hut previously was then blindfolded and led to the entrance of the hut. He entered and, with his groping hand, touched one of the stretchers. It was the corpse on this particular stretcher that was chosen to lie in State in Westminster Abbey.

Another account (page 17, British Butchers and Bunglers of World War One by Dr John Laffin [published in 1988 by Sutton Publishing Limited]), 'As the war ended there came the poetic idea of the "Unknown Warrior", the victim who would forever represent all the dead servicemen of the war. A blindfolded British Officer "of very high rank" - a general, in fact - was led into a hut containing the remains of six unidentified soldiers brought from the various battlefronts. He then groped about alone until he touched a coffin. This was the one taken back to Westminster Abbey and buried with all the honours that the nation could provide'. The event was a symbolism of sacrifice at its best, a magnificent idea. It was also entirely fitting. Blinkered generals, blind to the realities of war, had caused the shocking casualties. It was appropriate that they then should choose the man to represent all the soldiers who had been butchered.

And yet another account (pages 8-9 Chapter 1 *A Great Day for Westminster Abbey, 'The Age of Illusion'* by Ronald Blythe, Oxford University Press).

'... After the coffins had been laid side by side, everybody concerned with the operation up until this stage retired to a distance and an officer who had never been inside the hut previously was blindfolded and led to the door. He entered and his groping hand touched a coffin. And so was chosen the poor nameless flesh which would be followed through the streets of London by George V, the King-Emperor, on foot, and interred with every pomp and dignity known to the State in Westminster Abbey'.

But another more detailed account - addressed to the Editor of the Daily Sketch Newspaper in November 1939 is that of former Brigadier-General M Black, who wrote as follows:

Sir,

From time to time accounts have been published purporting to relate how and by whom the Unknown Warrior's body was selected in France for burial in Westminster Abbey on November 11th, 19 years ago. I should like to give here the authentic account of what took place.
In October, I received notification from the War Office that King George V had approved the suggestion and the proposal that the burial should be in Westminster Abbey on November the 11th . I issued instructions that the body of a British Soldier, which it would be impossible to identify, should be brought in from each of the four battle areas - the Aisne, the Somme, Arras and Ypres - on the night of November 7th and placed in the chapel of St Pol. The party bringing each body was to return at once to its area, so that there should be no chance of their knowing on which the choice fell.

Reporting to my headquarters office at St. Pol, at midnight on November 7th, Col. Gell, one of my staff, announced that the bodies were in the chapel and the men who had brought them had gone... The four bodies lay on stretchers, each covered by a Union Jack; in front of the altar was the shell of the coffin which had been sent from England to receive the remains. I selected one, and with the assistance of Col. Gell, placed it in the shell; we screwed down the lid. The other bodies were removed and reburied in the military cemetery outside my headquarters at St. Pol.

I had no idea even of the areas from which the body I selected had come; no one else can know it... The shell, under escort was sent to Boulogne... The next morning, carried by the pall-bearers who were selected from NCOs of the British and Dominion troops it was placed on a French military wagon and taken to Boulogne Quay where a British Destroyer was waiting... six barrels of earth from the Ypres Salient were put on board to be placed in the tomb at Westminster Abbey so that the body should rest in the soil on which so many of our troops gave up their lives.

Then HMS *Verdun* moved off, a guard of honour of Bluejackets at 'the Present' carrying that symbol which for so many years, and especially during the last few months, has meant so much to us all.

Yours etc.

M Black

Kendal, Cumbria Nov. 1939

But there remains one more account, the one that follows:

In the Public Record Office are kept certain documents relating to this historic event. The Vehicle Work Tickets in respect of each of the four ambulances involved in the transporting of the remains of the four servicemen. These were authorised journeys to expressed locations

(a)	Bázentin Le Petit (Somme area) - St. Pol	RETURN
(b)	Flesquie?es (Cambrau area) - St. Pol	RETURN
(c)	Gheluvelt (Ypres area) - St. Pol	RETURN
(d)	Monchy-le-Preux (Arras area) - St. Pol	RETURN

Thus, it can be assumed that all four ambulance parties involved knew of each other's destinations, at different times, since they belonged to the same unit, namely 45th Field Ambulance. One authorising officer signed all four work tickets.

Employed at the GHQ St. Pol were several Other Ranks employed on routine duties, such as the unloading of the plain coffin of English pine delivered on the 8th November 1920 and placed by them in the chapel. The two Other Ranks involved in this task were Cpl. Alfred Beasley. Formerly of the 2nd Bn Middlesex Regiment, and Pte. Lionel McDermott, formerly of the 6th Cameron Highlanders, both Regular Soldiers, involved in the Battle of Neuve Chapelle, Flanders 10-13 March 1915 and the Battle of Looe, northern France on 25 September 1915 respectively. After the removal of the three bodies of the servicemen not selected by Brigadier-General Black, they were involved in the re-interment of these remains in the military cemetery at St. Pol. Then, later, told to dispose of the remaining wooden stretcher on which the remains of the chosen body had once lain. It was during this task that Cpl. Beasley discovered a small blackened circular shaped piece of human bone from the body concealed in between the wooden slat cladding of the stretcher. He retained this find and told no one of it except Pte. McDermott. They broke up the stretcher and believed it was subsequently used as fire-wood within the camp precincts.

The item found by Beasley was carefully wrapped by him in a piece of cloth and sealed in an empty oblong tobacco tin and kept by him as a memento of the historic occurrence.

Contrary to what Brigadier-General Black and others thought about the impossibility of identification of the body chosen, later described by him, as being 'mere bones', many of the Other Ranks in the command were aware of the significance of the events set in motion by the various orders from Brigade HQ. Particularly, was this so in respect of the party selected to escort the coffin and its poor, sad, contents to Boulogne on the following day, the 8th November 1920.

These forming this party were:

(i) Company Sergeant Major Donald Bell, Royal Army Service Corps, 2 Brigade 8th Division
(ii) Sergeant T Keane, Royal Engineers, 54 Field Coy. RE 3 Brigade, Guards Division 5th Army
(iii) Lance Bombadier C Braithwaite, Royal Field Artillery, 4 Brigade 18 th Division 2nd Army
(iv) Trooper L Storre, Australian Light Horse, 4th Brigade, 4th Australian Division
(v) Private L Jessop, 18th (W. Ontario) Battalion, 4th Brigade 2nd Canadian Division
(vi) Private G Edwards, 97th Machine Gun Company, Machine Gun Corps
(vii) Rifleman J Harvey, 1/21st London (1st Surrey Rifles) 142 Brigade, 47th (London) Division

As Ronald Blythe writes in his book A Great Day for *Westminster Abbey - The Age of Illusion*, these companions of the body were humble enough - but, once at Boulogne, the superb elevation of their charge began. However, what has remained unreported for so long are the details of the military background and wartime experience of the party chosen to accompany Brigadier-General Black's 'mere bones' of a body to its final resting place.

Company Sergeant Major Bell, Military Medal, Mons Star, 1914-1919 War Medal, General Service Medal, a former member of the 11th West Surrey Regiment, 1st Division, British Expeditionary Force, later fought throughout the Somme battles from July to November 1916, after taking part in the battles at Mons and Ypres in 1914/15. Wounded and downgraded, but secured a transfer to the RASC.

In the battle of Gheluvelt, Ypres on the 31st October 1914, as a Lance Corporal, he was the sole surviving Non Commissioned Officer of 'D' Company 1st West Surrey Regiment. Of the 850 members of the Battalion, only one junior officer, and 32 other ranks survived.

Sgt. Keane, in September 1916 moved with his unit to High Wood on the Somme and saw hundreds of the British Infantry dead, lying in rows like corn that had been mowed down. The smell was awful and countless flies smothered the faces of the dead.

The dead lay so thick that the Company horses could not avoid running over them. The sight of these troops mown down by machine guns remained constantly with him and convinced him of the utter futility of war and the egotism of the senior officers who bungled in their methods at the expense of the lives of countless brave men. Lance Bombadier C Braithwaite R. A had once been a member of a firing squad detailed to execute a young soldier who, allegedly, was guilty of cowardice for which death was the ultimate penalty. The offender shot had been a good soldier up to the point of his desertion, but could take no more after seeing several of his Field Gun Team killed by a barrage of German 8" Howitzer Shells during counter-battery fire.

Trooper L Stone, Australian Light Horse had fought in the Gallipoli Campaign between 25th April 1915 and January 1916 where the casualties totalled about 205,000, including nearly 26,000 Australian casualties of whom over 7,500 were killed. The entire campaign achieved nothing.

Pte. L Jessop, 18th Bn. 2nd Canadian Division took part in the capturing of Vimy Ridge, Passchendaele when between 4th and 9th April 1917 the Canadian Troops suffered 11,000 casualties, he being one of the less severely wounded.

Pte. G Edwards 97th Machine Gun Company, 5th Division, served as a Vickers Machine Gunner on the Somme in July 1916 when five of the six-man gun team were killed. He, alone, survived wounded and dug out of a sap. Also served as a Machine Gunner in the Tank Attack on Fleur in the same battle.

Rfm. J Harvey 1/21st London (1st/4th Surrey Rifles), 47th Division, took part in the Battle of High Wood on the Somme when his brother was killed on 15th September 1916. Subsequently, the 47th Division was officially criticised for its 'lack of push' and its G.O.C. dismissed for 'wanton waste of men' entrusted to his command. The Division had lost over 4,500 men to secure an advance of about 100 yards of the German trench - every inch had cost a life.

These, then, were the seasoned and disillusioned men chosen to accompany the remains of a fellow soldier in an army ambulance to Boulogne.

At Boulogne, the British Destroyer, HMS *Verdun*, lay alongside the quay. The ship (during the night) had brought from England, a great oak coffin, weighing almost two-hundredweight. Two British undertakers, Mr Noakes and Mr Sowerbutts, placed the plain pine coffin, unopened, inside the casket of English oak, then secured the lid and sealed it.

The casket was placed on a French military wagon, drawn by six black horses and, with great and moving dignity to the strains of Chopin's *'Funeral March'*, taken to the dockside on the Quai Carnot and taken aboard HMS *Verdun* and accorded the naval honours normally accorded to an admiral.

Prior to the departure of the vessel, six barrels of earth taken from the Ypres Salient had been delivered to Westminster Abbey to be placed in the tomb so that the body should rest in soil on which so many troops had died. A man who had been nothing and was now to be everything had a funeral convoy of six destroyers with flags at the half-mast, to escort it to Dover where it received a Field Marshal's salute of nineteen guns fired from the castle. From Dover it travelled in a specially fitted saloon carriage to London where it rested overnight in a temporary chapel at Victoria Station. On the following morning, 11th November, pallbearers arrived to attend the corpse on its journey across the city. In attendance were Admirals Merex, Beatty, Jackson, Sturdee and Madden; Field Marshals French, Haig, Methuen, Wilson and Generals Home and Byng. Air-Marshal Trenchard followed alone.

At the Abbey, the grave had been dug just inside the west entrance, and, after committal it was filled with the earth from the Ypres Salient. A very large slab of Tornai marble was laid over it.

For a brief time it bore a simple inscription 'An Unknown Warrior'. But, further nitpicking occurred, on this occasion by the Dean of Westminster. Dean B Sides insisted that 'that in future time (1970) people will want to know who the Unknown Warrior was' and so compiled the many-worded inscription that it has to this day.

But, still the nitpicking went on when, later in 1921, the present black marble slab from Belgium replaced the Tornai marble slab. Mr S I Levy, Principal of the Liverpool Hebrew School, wrote to the Dean regarding one of the texts insisted upon by the Dean.

The text was 'In Christ shall all be made alive.' Principal Levy wondered if the Unknown Warrior might have been of the Jewish faith and, in which case, the line in question did not appear to meet the spiritual destinies of both Jew and Gentile.

The Dean replied that it was not outside the bounds of possibility that the Unknown Warrior might have been a Moslem - or a Mormon - 'we cannot hope to please everybody' he wrote. It all came to nothing, however, High Anglican tact remained firm.

Some forty-one years after this correspondence between the Dean and Principal Levy, a Maurice Hugh Frederick Wilkins, born in 1916, a New Zealand-born British Biophysicist who, with James Watson, Francis Crick and Rosalind Franklin, discovered the structure and DNA (deoxyribonucleic acid), shared the 1962 Nobel Prize with Watson and Crick (Franklin died before the award was presented). Genetic finger printing via DNA profile became possible. So there were still eight years to go before the Dean's prognostication about people wanting to know who the Unknown Warrior was. It now became, perhaps, possible to obtain a DNA profile from the remains of the 'Unknown Warrior' if this was deemed necessary. There had been many voices raised in the 1920s deriding both Armistice Day and the interment of the Unknown Warrior.

George Bernard Shaw argued that the disabled drag down wages and the standard of work, and should not be employed at all industrially. The duty of the country is perfectly clear. These men were disabled in its service and should be supported unconditionally.

Another echoed view was 'I think all this business about the Unknown Warrior cheap and tawdry - I would rather have spent the money on employing some life warriors, I suppose I am not as sentimental as I ought to be.'

Beatrice Webb's acid comment was that Downing Street had been barricaded lest there should be yet another, and still more impressive public ceremony - the funeral of an assassinated Prime Minister!

Others thought that remembrance of the dead should be combined with positive action to aid the living.

Evelyn Waugh deplored the whole idea on principle and derided it 'as a disgusting idea of artificial nonsense and sentimentality'.

The *Daily Herald's* comment 'who organised this pageant? The people who prolonged the war and grew rich out of it and now dope the people emotionally'.

Siegfried Sassoon, the poet, was one of those sickened by what they saw as the sentiment and hypocrisy of the proposed ceremonies at the Cenotaph and the grave of the Unknown Warrior. He wrote the lines 'The Prince of Darkness at the Cenotaph Bowed. As he walked away I heard him laugh.' And, W H Auden, in his poem, *'The Horizontal Man'* contrasted the pious platitudes about honouring the returning soldiers - 'the vertical man' - with the reality of their post-war predicament. Britain gave honour - or so he claimed - only to the 'horizontal man' - the Unknown Soldier who had no further demands to make of the society he had died to protect. His still-living comrades were no longer needed and were now ignored.

Even in 1916 at a meeting of the French war-wounded, one of the number said 'Today we are welcome, but after the war no one will speak of us and work will be hard to find.'

In so many cases this proved to be true and even during the fighting, H G Wells, in a letter to 'The Times' had written of asserting the need to shake off 'the ancient trappings of throne and sceptre' and men who had seen 'cities pounded to rubble, men who with little aid or guidance from their own rulers have chased emperors from their thrones, are pretty fully disengaged at last, from the Englishman's old sense of immutable fixity in institutions which he may find irksome or worthless'.

Like the 'cities pounded to rubble' so were the lives of countless other survivors of the conflict. Widows, those who had lost their husbands, fathers, brothers, sons, those who had hoped to marry, those who supported and cared for the maimed in body and mind - The Great War did indeed exact a random harvest - little wonder it was called 'great' and the casualties, too:

	Officers	Other Ranks
Killed	37,876	620,829
Wounded	92,644	1,939,478
Missing or Prisoners	12,094	347,051
TOTAL	3,049,972	

And warring nations, each suffered accordingly:

Killed	Frenchmen	1,380,000
	Germans	1,935,000
	Russians	1,700,000
	British Empire	1,081,952
	United States	48,909
	Austro Hungarians	1,300,000
	Italians	615,000
	Romania	335,000
	Turkey	325,000
	Bulgarians	90,000
	Serbs	55,000

All the nations involved had civilian deaths, in some cases almost as high as the military ones - all nations had their widows and orphans - as a result of the inane conflict - and all nations had to learn their history afresh within the space of twenty years - mourning became almost commonplace - a national numbness at the senseless, needless slaughter.

It was against this background that those engaged in the conflict decided to go their different way - Isolationism, Revenge, Communism, Pacifism, Republicanism - were but some of the names given to national policies, adopted to safeguard their interests.

In Britain there was one family, the two sons and one daughter of former Cpl. Alfred Beasley, whose health had deteriorated as a result of his war service and wounds, who had watched him suffer a painful death. During his better days he had told his children about his find in St. Pol many years previously, and explained its possible connection to the 'Unknown Warrior' buried in Westminster Abbey. His eldest son, Charles Beasley, was given the small metal tin and its contents as he hoped to study medicine and was considered to be its suitable guardian. Eventually, Charles completed his medical studies and obtained a post as an assistant to Prof Hugh Morrice, a Dutch biophysicist and his staff at a well-known University. The team discovered the structure of Deoxyribonucleic acid (DNA) and shared the Nobel Prize in 1962.

Charles mentioned his father's memento to others engaged in the discovery and it was decided to subject the bone and its adhered particles to a DNA profile test - perhaps the first genetic finger print. Initially, the tests were not altogether positive, but later, it was established that the blood group obtained from minute blood specks and hair follicles, had a particular condition. The sickle-shaped red blood cells indicated a form of anaemia, termed sickle-cell disease. The disease often affects people of African descent.

Such a disease is thought to shorten life expectancy because of the chronic damage to the tissues. There was, therefore, a distinct possibility that the Unknown Soldier had been a coloured member of the Armed Forces, and perhaps even, in a Pioneer capacity, employed on the dangerous duties of conveying supplies etc - all part of the logistical demands of those in the front line. Such work was vital and the German artillery shelled many of the roads, tracks, paths used by General Service Wagons. Those killed were buried in the immediate vicinity and this entire area was later the scene of fierce fighting, before being captured by the Germans in their breakthrough in late March 1918.

It would be quite possible that the Unknown Warrior in Westminster Abbey is not 'a Mormon or a Moslem' but 'inside the bounds of possibility', might have a coloured member of the Armed Forces. Perhaps, if this is the case, the Church of England's High Anglican tact, as evidenced by Dean B Sides's remark, can still remain firm. The involvement of the Church's missionary arm, the Society for the Propagation of the Gospel in Foreign Parts in its use of slave labour to run its Codrington estate on Barbados between 1710 and 1834, needed far more than the apology for its culpability. The burial of one descended from an ancestor, who was a slave of the Church of England, in the hallowed precincts of Westminster Abbey, might ease the soul-searching and help bury the chains of the first holocaust.

But, whether it excuses the arrogance and pathological pride of the various army commanders on all sides responsible for the great slaughter in the Great War, is indeed, another matter. An apology there is still to be forthcoming.

Church's slavery apology 'is not enough'

Descendants of plantation workers want more than just a word

Slavery is not something you can say sorry for and then be done with it

An unhappy reminder of complicity in a tragedy

The Daily Telegraph. Saturday 11th February 2006, reproduced below.

Church's slavery apology 'is not enough

Descendants of plantation workers want more than just a word
LISA Codrington knew her ancestors were Anglicans like her and that, almost two centuries ago, they were slaves. But she did not realise until recently that they were slaves of the Church of England.

The clue is in her name: Codrington. Slaves of British planters often took the name of their masters and, until 1710, Miss Codrington's fore-bears lived on the Codrington plantation in Barbados.

After that date, as she discovered for herself a year or two before the apology in this week's General Synod made it clear to the rest of us, the Codrington lands, and the hundreds of slaves on them, became Church property.

The Codrington slaves, men like Devonshire Codrington, born in 1776 and Lisa's many-times great-grandfather, did not become free until 1834, when the Church, like all slave-owners, was forced to release them.

Anglican culpability in the Caribbean. slave trade can be traced back at least to 1710, when the planter Christopher Codrington died, leaving his 300-acre Barbados plantations to the Church's newly-established Society for the Propagation of the Christian Religion in Foreign Parts (SPG).

So Miss Codrington and her family are well-placed to comment on the Church's apology. "It's a good start," said the 28-year-old actress and playwright, who was born in, Winnipeg, Canada, of Barbadian parents and now works as an actress in Toronto.

"But is that all? I don't know how I feel about the apology until I hear every thing about it. Is it involving reparation? Is it involving further work, further education by the Church?"

Mention of reparation will send shivers down ecclesiastical spines, because many institutions, including the British Government, have worried about apologising for slavery in case they are asked to put their money where their mouths are. "The more they do the better they do," she added. "Slavery is not something you can say sorry for and then be done with it."

Miss Codrington has been in Barbados for a month, researching a play about pre-emancipation life, with her mother Hughlene.

Mrs Codrington left Barbados for Canada in the 1970s, but her daughter has been back several times, fascinated by how much detail she can find about her slave ancestry.

She feels that the Church of England will have got away lightly if nothing more than words come from its bout of self-flagellation. "People have gotten worse [punishments] for doing less," Miss Codrington said. She started to think about her ancestry when a teacher at her drama school asked her to write a monologue "in an accent" and she chose to do it using her mother's native Bajan dialect.

But she has not leapt straight into a quest to lay the blame for her ancestors' sufferings. "I am at the investigative stage right now," she said. "I am the sort of person who likes to understand why things are the way they are."

"I realised that some. of these things, like names and faiths, may not have, been necessarily matters of choice. They may have been imposed. For me it's more important to figure out why' and try to understand it than to get angry." In north-east Load Miss Codrington's aunt, Devenish-Scott, 48, an educational consultant, had not heard about the Church's apology until told by The Daily Telegraph.

Although a Pentecostalist rather than an Anglican, she inclines to be forgiving of the Church of England's past sins towards her family. "I know that the Church, unlike the rest of the plantocracy in Barbados, established the first schools for black children there. "I am not saying that excuses what they did though, and it would be right for them to provide more now for the families of people who suffered. I don't think a lot of people knew then, and would be appalled, but it seems like an appropriate time to apologise".

In Barbados, Woodville Marshall, emeritus professor of history at the University of the West Indies, said the Church's sins over Codrington were those of omission more than commission. "They had professional planters to run the place," he said. "The Church didn't play an active role, because they were more interested in the receipts."

After the plantation was left to the SPG, its slaves were branded on the chest with the word "society", to remind everyone that these were slaves of the Lord. In 1740, 30 years after the Church took over, four out of every 10 slaves bought by the plantation died within three years. "Most people in Barbados are not too troubled by these issues," Prof Marshall said, "It was not so much the SPG that the Church should be apologising for as the activities of the individual parsons who kept plantations and slaves for sheer profit."

"The bicentenary of the abolition of the slave trade, which falls next year, has prompted an uncomfortable bout of soul-searching in the Church of England.

While it has been at pains to highlight the role of reformers in ending the trade, it has been less anxious - until Wednesday's General Synod debate - to acknowledge its own involvement. Most obviously, the Church's missionary arm, the Society for the Propagation of the Gospel in Foreign Parts, used slave labour to run its Codrington estate on Barbados between 1710 and 1834. The society's governing body included Archbishops of Canterbury, one of whom wrote in 1760: "1 have long lamented that the Negroes in our plantation decrease and new supplies become necessary continually.

"Surely this proceeds from some defect, both of humanity and even of good policy. But we must take things as they are at present." Not all clerics were so accepting. Dr Beilby Porteus, a Bishop of London, spoke out against the trade and attempted to improve conditions for the slaves.

But the Church's general attitude reflected that of the prevailing culture, which assumed that slavery was part of the order that God had ordained on earth for centuries. In the 18th century the onus was on opponents of the slave trade to show that it was against the will of God, and only when abolitionists were beginning to gain ground did supporters tend to respond.

One attempt was a 1788 pamphlet by Raymund Harris, a Church of England clergyman, entitled Scriptural Researches on the Licitness of the Slave Trade, Showing its Conformity with the Principles of Natural and Revealed Religion.

The abolitionist movement, which was largely inspired by Quakers, Methodists, and evangelical Christians, began to turn the tide when ideas of social justice became more widely accepted."

SELECT BIBLIOGRAPHY AND SOURCES

The Unknown Soldier - Neil Hansen, Transworld Publishing - Doubleday

British *Butchers and Bunglers of World War One* - Professor John Laffin, Sutton Publishing

The Somme - Peter Hart, Weidenfield and Nicholson

Scient Desk Reference - Macmillan, The New York Public Library, USA

A History Of The Twentieth Century - Volume One 1900-1933 - Sir Martin Gilbert, Harper Collins Publishers

Voices and Images of the Great War

Bury The Chains (The British Struggle to Abolish Slavery), Adam Hochschild, Macmillan

The Daily Telegraph Sat. 11th February 2006, Page 4

'LACHRYMA CHRISTI' (THE TEARS OF CHRIST)

PART ONE

LIFE

CHAPTER ONE

The invisible tendrils of a January wind explored the cold grey platforms of Rome Railway Station and found themselves rebuffed by the kit bag, field-service packs and other army equipment of Corporal Charles Easton who crouched in their centre. The year was 1945, the third year of the Italian Campaign and, Easton, one of the few persons on the station late that night, awaited the arrival of a troop train which was to take him to Florence to rejoin his Infantry Regiment fighting the German and Italian Armies high up in the Appenine Mountains just below Bologna.

He had spent the better part of the previous day travelling up to Rome from the Infantry Base Depot to which he had been posted after being wounded in a battle near Lake Trasimeno in late summer the year before. He was no stranger to the Rome area, having slogged along the dusty roads to reach the Eternal City after the bitter fighting beneath the brooding heights of Monte Cassino. Throughout the four long Cassino battles between September 1943 and June 1944 in muddy winter and arid summer, his battalion had attacked repeatedly only to be repulsed by the formidable enemy whose shock troops were from the German 1st Parachute Division.

His battalion had suffered severe losses and he wondered how he had endured the artillery bombardments, the freezing nights and the scorching heat of high summer when the dust and poisonous reek of high explosives clogged the nostrils and the mind itself. The courage and fortitude of his companions in his Section had been a mutual link between them. Without it he felt certain that he would have been unable to cope in the frequent night attacks during the winter. He had detested slithering in the wet mud, like the over-burdened mules accompanying them. Following dirty-ribboned tapes, marking the minefields laid by the enemy in pathways through the rocky outcrops, they had fought ever-upwards over the flint-hard mountain face. Forever with them were the ear-splitting cracks of the detonating shells, echoing and re-echoing in the dark mountain vastness.

Cold, wet, often hungry and always scared and weary, they had eventually fought their way to victory. How long ago it all was, he reflected, and yet here again it was night with the cold winds of winter chilling his extremities. He disliked these shrivelling winds; harbingers of death he called them, when the defences of the old, frail and mortally sick were finally overcome. At twenty-four years of age, he had seen too much of death and the useless sacrifice of both the brave and the craven alike, to delude himself as to the meaning of life in wartime. It was merely a case of survival until the quiet days of peace returned.

His stay in hospital with a gun-shot wound in the fleshy part of his right hip had not been excessive. Once the two bright red-lipped wounds had finished suppurating and began to heal, he was discharged to a convalescent camp to make room for the more recent casualties. The camp had been pleasantly situated near the Adriatic Sea and, by late winter, he had fully recovered to be passed medically fit for return to his unit.

He had arrived in Rome shortly before midnight and his enquiries of the Railway Transport Staff had elicited little firm information, save that the arrival of the Northbound troop train was expected shortly after dawn on the following day.

Advised either to avail himself of the waiting rooms in the station, or to obtain overnight accommodation in one of the nearby Transit Barracks, he had chosen to remain in his military cocoon of equipment on the platform. Drawing the collar of his greatcoat up about his ears and pulling his forage cap further over his rebellious mop of hair, he snuggled down to try to get what rest he could before the travelling rigours of the morrow. He dozed rather than slept and frequently banged his army boots together to engender some warmth into his cold feet.

As if from a distance, he heard a voice calling to him. With his gloved hands he brushed his eyes, blinked himself into wakefulness, and saw the person addressing him. He saw a girl of about eighteen years of age, very small and delicate of build with a young, pinched face peering out from what appeared to be an old fur coat at least a size too big for her. Her brown hair had natural waves, one of which fell interrogatively over her forehead. Her flat-heeled, sandal-type shoes protruded slightly from the hem of the coat. In a mixture of Italian and English, she spoke to him.

'Voi, soldata, niente train this night.' She glanced up the empty ribbons of railway track as if to make him understand her remark.

His command of Italian, although not over-strong grammatically, was sufficient for him to explain to her that he was aware that there was no train at present, but that there would be one arriving in the morning. His fairly fluent command of her language and use of its pleasantries of speech when addressing her as 'a dear young lady', obviously delighted her, and her rewarding smile warmed him inwardly.

He knew instantly and instinctively that she was probably one of the many girls who, because of the appalling difficulties in wartime Italy and the distress of the civilian population, sought the companionship of the troops, whatever their nationality. In return for army rations or other foodstuffs which they took home to their families or relatives, they gave all they had to give - themselves. Many of the younger girls were without parents who had been killed in the fighting or bombing attacks, and were looked after, as far as possible, by a distant relative. In the hard, uncompromising times, he had seen even small children already skilled in the stealing and cadging arts and generally living on their wits. It was a side of War he loathed and hated, having been an orphan himself from a very early age. The Army had proved to be a refuge of sorts for him and, although he had been a regular soldier for over six years and was a comparatively seasoned campaigner, he detested this part of the War. He was never indifferent to the plight of the refugees and the bombed-out families, whatever their nationalities. Invariably, he had doled out some of army canteen purchases to the children, their profuse, genuine thanks and their broad grubby grins as they clutched the odd chocolate bar and bore it triumphantly off home, made the war bearable for him. Children always found the thin side of his soldierly cynicism and he minded it not one bit.

His thoughts returned to the present. The girl's small, white face with its wide brown eyes looking steadily at him - how often he had seen that look before and implied its meaning. Rummaging in his army pack, he found the rations he had drawn at the Depot to last him the journey and offered them to her. She made as if to accept them but first asked if he had sufficient food left for himself.

'Oh, lots', he replied, laughingly, to dissuade further enquiry.
'Let me see?' she said disbelievingly, peering child-like into his army pack. She glanced up quickly, having completed her

inspection of its contents. 'You haven't any left', she said, almost incredulously.

'Well, I can get some more tomorrow', he replied quickly. 'Don't worry, you take these home to your family.' As he spoke, he stuffed the loaf of bread, small amounts of tea, sugar and coffee, two tins of corned beef and other items into a small sandbag, wrapped the bundle as securely as possible and placed it in her arms. He then pulled his greatcoat closely about him and prepared to settle down amidst his equipment. She remained still and quiet watching him and, without a word, walked away. He glanced at her retreating figure and she turned and smiled enigmatically before her small figure disappeared from his sight.

With a warm, contented smile on his face, he pummelled his place of rest into a state of semi-acceptability. The cold brass butt of his rifle made a dull clanking sound on the concrete platform every time it slipped down through his cradled arms. With his hands stuffed deep within his overcoat pockets, his cap pulled well down over his eyes, he endeavoured to doze away the waiting hours. Engrossed in his bedding-down activity, he failed to hear the returning footsteps of his former companion. Suddenly she appeared before him, dressed as before, but without the foodstuffs he had previously given to her.

'I haven't anything else', he remarked, jocularly, turning himself away from her and squirming into a more comfortable position.

'No, no', she protested vehemently, and continued, 'my Aunt has sent me to tell you that you must come to our flat and not sleep in the cold in the Railway Station.'

'You must have a very understanding Aunt,' he replied, making no attempt to accept the invitation.

She ignored his reply and tried to pull him to his feet. 'Come, quickly', she insisted, her features set quite determinedly.

'Do you want me to come?' he queried lightly.

'Of course I do, otherwise I would not have returned to fetch you', she replied, crossly.

He rose suddenly, expertly slung the packs and equipment over his greatcoat, buckled his belt, hoisted his kit-bag on one shoulder and slung his rifle sling over the other shoulder. The rapidity of his actions and his instant decision to do her bidding, obviously pleased his companion, for her look of pouted determination had been replaced by one of almost maternal concern.

He was at least a head taller than the girl and with his equipment festooned about him, he thought they must have looked an incongruous pair as they walked out of the Station. She remonstrated at his fast pace, which he slackened as she placed an arm within one of his crooked elbows. He listened attentively to her directions, and, during their brief walk, he learned that her name was Nicola and that she lived with her Aunt in a small flat in the immediate vicinity of the railway station. After their mutual exchange of names, she thereafter called him 'Carlo', which, she solemnly informed him was the Italian for his own name. Although already aware of this fact, he made no mention of it, and permitted her to correct his frequent mispronunciation of various words he used conversationally during their journey.

The streets were silent and dark and he presumed that some form of curfew was in existence. He glanced down at her small face and saw there a compound look of a young, innocent girl and a very worldly aware young lady. He was amused at first by the possessive care she displayed for him, but he realised very suddenly that such concern for his welfare had an underlying cause. It was much like the feelings he displayed when treating the wounds of men in his section during a particular action. Compassion and tenderness were very much evident in her feelings for him. He did not fully understand their significance, and it puzzled him a little.

He supposed it to be a sense of belonging very briefly in a way of living outside Army life, every nuance of the latter was known to him. This meeting was strange and unexpected - a brief strand of intermission in the web and warp of war - between a world-weary soldier and a young girl who had befriended him late on a cold winter's night and with whom he was now walking along still quiet streets beneath the vast darkness of the sky overhead.

CHAPTER TWO

Very quickly they reached a flight of a dozen stone steps which led to the block of flats in which she lived. The effects of previous bombing raids on the railway station and its locality were much in evidence. Doorways had been shored up with bone white pieces of wood, positioned almost like a series of Crucifixes. Large sheets of tarpaulin covered some of the bomb-blasted areas, but still to be seen were splintered windows, tile-less sections of the roof, mounds of brick and, everywhere, mortar dust. It was a depressing sight, but once they had entered the small kitchen of the flat with the welcoming glow provided by a wood fire and low watt electric lighting, he experienced a profound change of feeling. The girl's Aunt, a buxom woman of about fifty years of age, had prepared a meal of spaghetti and grated cheese and, on the white tablecloth, he saw spread out all the foodstuffs he had given to the girl. Nicola quickly removed her coat and helped him to take off his equipment. He was given hot water and a towel and sent into the small room leading from the kitchen in which to wash himself. As he combed his unruly hair into some semblance of order, he heard them talking together as to where he was to be placed at the table. He re-entered the room and tried to get them to eat without him for he knew how difficult it was for them to manage domestically day by day. His objections were tactfully and laughingly ignored and he soon found himself clean and glowing seated with them.

It was a simple meal made all the more pleasurable by the lateness

of the hour and their ready acceptance of him. Towards the end of the meal, the Aunt, who mothered him constantly, produced a bottle of strong red sweet wine which, she informed him, she had kept since Christmas. Three glasses were filled to the brim and they asked him to make a wish as it was a very special wine called, *'Lachryma Christi'*. He got to his feet and looked down on them warmly. 'I wish', he said, and then paused and smiled, 'that after the war is over, I shall come back to Rome and meet you both again'.
'Bravo, Carlo,' responded Nicola animatedly, clapping her small hands. The meal, and especially the wine, had a mellowing effect upon him and a fluency in their language he had not thought he possessed. His tales of Army life, its fortunes and misfortunes caused his companions much amusement as he assisted them to clear the table and wash and wipe the plates and glasses. Arrangements were then made for him to sleep in Nicola's room, and, since Nicola's Aunt made the suggestion, he presumed he would find a couch or bed in the room, in addition to Nicola's sleeping place. On entering her small room, which was sparsely furnished, he found but one bed with Nicola's fur coat serving as a coverlet. Perched on the two pillows was a rather bedraggled cuddly toy rabbit. 'That's Nicola's lucky charm', explained the Aunt as she left the room bidding them both a pleasant night's sleep.

The Aunt's ready acceptance of the sleeping arrangements at first puzzled him. He supposed, however, that in Wartime Italy, the normal strait-laced attitude to such situations was no longer rigidly held. When accommodation and the means to exist were scarce and difficult to find, possibly the moral implications possessed less significance.

Nicola had undressed quickly, slipped a nightdress over her head and was already snuggled down in the bed.

'Hurry up, Carlo,' she whispered, 'I'm cold'.

Despite his service background and the accepted vulgarity on occasion of barrack life, he was basically shy and reserved by nature and had never before in his life slept other than alone. The hard iron cots with equally hard mattresses had been his lot in the orphanages and in the various army barracks in which he had been quartered. In the Libyan Desert in previous campaigns, the hard unyielding sand had been his resting place beneath the velvet sky and, as an Infantryman in Italy, usually a trench with a groundsheet spread for protection covered him from the elements.

To hide his shyness, he turned his back towards Nicola and quickly undressed. As he removed his underclothes, Nicola, who was peeping above the edge of the sheets watching his every action, saw the harsh, red, barely-healed wounds on his hip.
'Oh, Carlo', she cried, and clambered across the bed and embraced him. Her arms about the tops of his shoulders held him protectively as she repeatedly brushed her lips and cheeks against his back. In one swift movement, she drew him into the bed and extinguished the light.

He lay still in the darkness, aware of the gradual warmth of their bodies so close together. He longed to hold her softness against him but, despite the wine he had drunk, he could not overcome his inhibitions. He found that his feelings for her, prompted by a sense of compassion and respect for her honesty and warm-heartedness, were such that he could not consider their relationship purely on a physical level. Something else was present - a tangible awareness between them that this was not simply a casual meeting in wartime between a soldier returning to the front line and a Roman girl, less virtuous perhaps than she might have been, had not the war occurred. Their meeting was to be far more than a mere fleeting romance - that he knew for certain.

In the close darkness, Nicola smiled knowingly. She, too, knew that something different had occurred in her life. Her previous existence with its casual affairs with unknown soldiers, never intense, never lasting and, sometimes, sordid and cheap, was never to return. She vowed it in her heart and mind and made a small silent prayer that her dream would, one day, come true. She turned away on her side and pressed herself warmly against him, her fingers lightly seeking and tracing his wounds as if to comfort the torn flesh and make it whole and smooth again. Her soft caresses made him tumescent and, although he tried to ease himself gently away from her, she pressed the more insistently against him, well aware of his unspoken need of her. Suddenly she turned and in an instant entered into his waiting arms, their lips meeting blindly and urgently. Much later he kissed her soft eyelids closed, brushed the spun strands of hair from her damp face and held her closely and fiercely until she slept - her face calm and free from passion. With the warmth and serenity of her presence he, too, slept, and her softness and love dispelled forever the cold previously ever-present loneliness within him.

CHAPTER THREE

Towards dawn's first light, wakefulness came. It was for him a natural reaction, for in the front line he and his comrades had always stood to and manned their dugouts to repel any dawn attacks by the enemy. Very few such attacks had ever developed, since the Germans, in the main, were strongly defence-minded and committed themselves usually to counter-attack to regain lost territory, or launched their own attacks at last light. However, he mused, old habits die hard, and he lay awake watching the first suffused light of the coming day seeping into the room. He looked down tenderly on Nicola, breathing lightly in the crook of his arm. Through the thin nightdress he saw the roseate hue marking her breasts, and felt her thin young arms holding him captive as if she too wished the moment of happiness to be never-ending. Her beauty for him came from within herself, it was incapable of definition and he knew only that she was the person for whom, either consciously or otherwise, he had been seeking all his life. It was far from being a case of mother-substitution, he knew himself to be too self-sufficient for such a need. The fact that they were different nationalities mattered not - the nature of their respective lives previous to their meeting was for him totally irrelevant. One could know many women or men physically and yet retain an inner purity. It was, he thought, all very much relative and human needs, as he knew too well, manifested themselves in so many diverse ways - food, sustenance, shelter, ego needs, affection and, always, love and companionship. All humanity required them in varying degrees for successful fulfilment of themselves.

She stirred within his arms, her body unconsciously making its silent demands of him. Very tenderly and lovingly, he placated them, and wordless and open-eyed, they lay together for a magical non-physical instant of time never to be lost.
'I love you, Carlo', she said, breathing the words into his lips. He lifted a light wisp of her hair from across her eyes and kissed briefly her forehead. 'I know', he replied simply. 'And I, you, young Nicola.'

There was an unspoken understanding between them that what had occurred was but a beginning and that it would be endless, despite all the trials and tribulations that would undoubtedly follow their mutual decision to belong simply to each other. Already, vaguely formulated plans were revolving within his mind and he knew he need not voice them for they were understood by Nicola. Their former life pattern, with its empty loneliness was behind them. There was a sharing and caring future to be considered. He knew the remainder of the war had to be endured and that he and his comrades were about to join in the very last battle of the Italian campaign. He hoped desperately that he would survive the attacks yet to be made for he now had so much to live for.

They dressed and washed quickly and ate hurriedly the meagre breakfast Nicola's Aunt had prepared for them. It was but coffee and bread, but it was their first breakfast together. He thanked her Aunt for her kindness and received a warm embrace from her. She, too, knew that she need no longer fear for Nicola's future and that one day he would return. So little had been said, but so much had happened during the few brief hours following his arrival at the small bomb-scarred flat. Once outside, the cold early winds sought them and Nicola snuggled closer to the roughness of his greatcoat, her head against his shoulder. Since they were in good time to catch the train, Nicola took him to the Treviso Fountain where, as instructed by her, he tossed in a coin to ensure his return to the Eternal City. As the coin slid crab-wise through the water to the marbled bottom, she reached up and kissed him; just to make his wish come true, as she explained.

Oblivious to the waking world around them, they sauntered slowly through the empty streets making plans. The beauty of Rome as a city was made more beautiful for him by his companion. The impressive squares, churches, statues and fountains seemed to have been built many years ago simply to make this particular morning with Nicola memorable. Her own beauty surpassed everything he saw. Perhaps one day, he thought, they might wander again through the city with time their ally instead of their enemy. As they walked he told her of the arrangements he would make to send to her his accredited army pay and a weekly amount to follow which she and her Aunt were to use to augment their income and for any other purpose they chose. Nicola, too, entered into the bargain by promising to put aside a little of the money she earned as a part-time helper in a local cafeteria. His remonstrance that such sacrifice was unnecessary failed to dissuade her and she remained adamant that it would help in starting their life together. She finally convinced him of the soundness of her decision by telling him that she could then afford the railway or bus fare to Florence or some other city or town behind the front line, where they might meet if he obtained local leave of absence from his unit. So intense became their mutual concern for each other during their discussion of the time they would be apart, that eventually they both laughed at the ridiculousness of the situation.

'Here we are', he said finally, 'Having met but yesterday arguing like a couple of long standing.'

She nodded excitedly in agreement, 'Yes', she replied, 'isn't it

wonderful. I'm sure we shall be like this for always, and very happy too.'
'You are incorrigible', he spluttered, laughingly in English, and of course, had to translate the word to her as best he could.

The cavernous coldness of the station as they entered gripped him tightly within his body. The troop train, metallic and impersonal, stood alongside the platform with the usual military bustle and activity present. Officers were checking their drafts of men and Non-Commissioned Officers allocating particular unit personnel to specific carriages. Seemingly aloof from it all were the Military Policemen controlling the troops boarding the train. He shrugged his army pack higher on his shoulders before taking Nicola suddenly into his arms and kissing her fiercely. She clung tightly to him, her smallness pressed close as if to defend him from whatever lay ahead. 'Goodbye, Carlo, my love,' she breathed as their lips parted and then clasped his cold hands within her own. He raised them and rested them gently against his cheek as their eyes met. 'Goodbye, Nicola,' he said quietly. 'I shall write to you every day in my best Italian.' She nodded in reply, her crooked little smile concealing the emotion within her. He swallowed hard as he turned away and handed his travelling documents to the Transport Staff before boarding the train.

CHAPTER FOUR

Quickly he thrust his equipment on the luggage rack and then stood by the carriage door looking at her distant, forlorn figure. Love and tenderness for her welled within him and momentarily he gave thought to leaving the train and rejoining her. At that moment he felt the train jerk suddenly, heard the sound of closing doors and, with a convulsive series of tugs, the train slowly gathered motion. His eyes never left her figure and he remained looking in her direction even when the station walls and adjoining houses slid into his line of vision and she could no longer be seen.

Serious of face, he entered the crowded compartment, sorted his kit into a reasonably ordered state and then sat back in his seat. Gradually, the countryside came into view, farms tucked away in the hillsides, steep, snow-covered hills, rivers grey and brown in spate and, everywhere in the background, the dreaded grey, snow-capped mountainous chain. In every vista he saw the small, lovely child-like face of Nicola and he knew he loved her with every fibre of his being. The memory of their few hours together sent a joyous feeling surging through him - a sensuous, mentally satisfying mood of reflection settled upon him. Occasionally he would enter into conversation with the other troops in the carriage, most of whom were replacements and had never before been in the front line. Seeing the African Star ribbon on his battledress tunic and his Corporal's chevrons, they sought his advice and opinion on various military matters to do with the campaign. All appeared a trifle apprehensive, but endeavoured to conceal their true thoughts by small acts of bravado. He warmed to them, but continually his thoughts returned to Nicola and his plans for their future together.

Although aware of the official line on non-fraternisation, he dismissed it with a mental shrug. He and Nicola would be married soon. Whether in Italy or elsewhere, did not really matter. His regular service engagement of seven years in the Army had but a few months to run and, although he knew his services would be retained for the duration of the war, he knew he would be one of the first servicemen to be demobilised. With his experience of the years of travel and discomfort, there would prove to be very few difficulties he would not be able to overcome. He thought of his first letter to her and wished that his studies of Italian had not neglected the written word. His oral command of the language was such that he had been offered a post in the Battalion Intelligence Section, but he had declined the post in order to remain with his Section with whom he had endured so much. His services as an Interpreter had always been in demand, especially when his Platoon had been resting out of the front line. With an ingenious use of local dialects, learned by ear, he had obtained wine, eggs, fresh vegetables, even the odd chicken, from the intensely suspicious farming communities high up in the hills and mountainous area. His exchange of army rations had always been done on a fair basis and he had kept rigidly to bargains struck. He liked the hardy mountain people. He never knew that many of his 'parishioners', as he called them, often spoke of him with affection and wished that one day, 'Carlo' would return with his infectious brand of humour and flippant indifference to the difficulties of life.

From his battledress he removed his Italian notebook and a very dog-eared English/Italian dictionary and, with references to it, began to compose his very first letter to Nicola. 'Cara Mia' might be his first salutation, he though, but then decided that 'My very own Nicola' would be much more acceptable.

As the day wore on, the scenery altered and soon the truly beautiful city of Florence came into view in its setting amidst the hills of Tuscany. But, ever deep in the background, was the grim-looking Appenine chain. The clouds obscured the peaks but he felt their cold hostility through his clothing. The train halted in some railway sidings where lines of drab coloured vehicles were drawn up awaiting their arrival. In the half light he and his colleagues were quickly marshalled into unit replacement formations and allotted transport. With several others, he clambered over the tailboard of a three-ton truck, helped stack their army equipment at the rear and along the sides of the truck's interior, caught the ration packs slung aboard each vehicle, and then settled down as comfortably as possible for the journey ahead. In each of the individual ration packs there was a small bar of chocolate and he removed his bar and placed it in his small haversack. It was for Nicola and he reflected that he might have amassed a small store of such bars by the time they met again. Later, as the trucks ground in slow gear up the twisting Borgo San Lorenzo road, he saw everywhere on the road sides the devastation caused by the recent shelling. Whole forests of once beautiful trees stood splintered and dead in shell-pocked desolation. Everywhere lay black and orange fire-gutted tanks and half-tracked vehicles. Tank turrets, once used by the enemy as strongpoints, and now blasted from the tenacious earth and concrete by shell-fire, pointed in crazy angles towards the darkening sky. Cruel barbs of rusty wire, packs, letters, shell-cases, ammunition boxes, helmets, rifles - the entire flotsam and jetsam of modern war was present, except the dead. They had been removed by Graves Registration personnel, ostensibly for moral and ethical purposes, but he could not escape the thought that the speedy removal of the dead had morale-boosting implications.

The young soldiers with him, some but 19 years of age, gaped open-mouthed and stared wide-eyed at the fought-over battlefield. This was war at its bitterest - a fierce, brave, stubborn enemy skilled in the so-called arts of war, but, although the German Troops did not accept it, they were already beaten by their dogged adversaries. Then there were the elements - utterly indifferent to both sides. The frozen mountain winds, the snow, the steel-tipped lances of rain lashing all, quite indiscriminately.

Long before the others in the truck became aware of the sound, he heard the thudding of the artillery in the gun lines. The reports reverberated like thunder along the mountain ridges and he weakened momentarily in his bowels. It had always been this way, first a marked loosening of control and acute physical fear, and then, slowly, the disciplined tightening of nerve and sinew. Finally, but, gradually, the forced humorous cynicism born of experience and the need to hide one's innermost thoughts and feelings. This time, however, he wished not only to survive the coming battle, but also to remain unwounded and to return to Nicola and life itself. His introspective thoughts were intruded upon frequently by his companions and he found himself explaining the difference between the heavier 105mm guns and the medium 25 pdr guns in the artillery lines. He indicated to them the mule-lines and camouflaged ammunition dumps in the rear areas and generally provided a sense of security for the younger soldiers. His companions became quiet as the military activity lessened and they approached the front line area itself.

'It's a bit lonely up here, Cpl', one youngster remarked, and the truth behind the lad's statement intrigued him.

'Well, we are a sort of select company up here', he replied with an understanding grin. 'We call it the sharp end, but it has its compensations', he added mysteriously. 'Such as what, Corporal?' queried another soldier, insistently.

'No drill parades, kit inspections, regimental guards and that sort of thing', he replied. He left unsaid any mention of the discomfort, fatigues, night patrols and the ever-present feeling of revealing one's fear. These things they would learn soon enough for themselves; why disillusion their youthful confidence and optimism, he reasoned. Perhaps in time they would acquire the knowledge that the way to survive both mentally and physically was to think of oneself as possessing a personal immunity; that others would be wounded or killed, but not oneself. It was a ridiculous assumption but, strangely enough, seemed to work in some cases. He had found that it was of paramount importance to avoid developing a moral insensibility amidst the brutality of modern war. The intense comradeship amongst those actually fighting helped considerably in this respect. He had witnessed the tender care given unstintingly to the wounded and the dying; had helped steady the stretchers harnessed to the mules as they made their stumbling way down the mountainside to the Regimental Aid Posts. He had seen the consideration given to the children, women, the old and infirm driven from their homes by the ravaging shell-fire and bombing attacks. Altogether, he had seen too much of the stupidity of war and knew that in the end there were 'no winners'; all were losers in some way or another. What was it a Mr Jones, a Welshman once said 'war is the sport of kings and the trade of hired assassins'.

His further reflections were cut short as the truck whined to a halt. Through the open canvas canopy of the vehicle he saw the deep layers of mud on the rutted road surface. The different tyre patterns of gun limbers and vehicles, hoof impressions of the mules, were all imprinted for an instant only before the bitterly cold winter rain washed them away.

The mist rolled down the mountain sides and added to the grey, discomforting picture, but within an hour he was with his former Section billeted in a shell-battered farmhouse. He caught up with the various happenings in his absence, noted the new faces and made the necessary acquaintances. Satisfying himself that all his men had eaten and had adequate shelter, he turned to his own affairs. He found he had been allotted a bunk on a heaped stack of old sacks on which he spread his groundsheet and blankets and settled down.

Within the room it was tolerably comfortable, the boarded-up windows having been covered with blankets and old sand bags. A wood fire blazed in the large open hearth and light was provided by hurricane lamps hanging from the beams. Before commencing his letter to Nicola, he glanced quickly at the various weapons held by the Section. Finding them all clean and serviceable, with a clear conscience, he began to write. With frequent references to his dictionary which tended to interrupt his train of thought, he soon completed the letter. He enclosed several Lira notes in the envelope and knew that the eventual delivery of the letter and its contents posed no difficulty since he had previously made arrangements with his colleagues in the Divisional Transport Section whose duties frequently took them to Rome to collect mail, rations and other items of freight.

CHAPTER FIVE

A week before his Section left reserve duties to return to the front line, he received Nicola's reply and his secret worries that all might not have been well with them were immediately dispelled when he read her opening lines. That she had couched them in simple Italian for his benefit was evident, as, too, was the love and affection she undoubtedly had for him. In every alternate paragraph she mentioned the fact that she longed for them to be together again with only her lucky rabbit for company. She gave him news of her Aunt's welfare, her own busy activities, and mentioned that she would be able to get to Florence whenever he could manage to obtain some leave. Apparently, her Aunt had arranged accommodation for them with relatives whose farm-cum-vineyard was but a short distance from Florence itself.

With this news warming him inside like a brazier, he returned, with his Section, to the front line. For two whole weeks they endured the elements and spasmodic shell-fire, but they were not called upon to mount any attacks. The bitter winter weather, with frequent heavy snow falls simply did not permit a resumption of the offensive. Until well into late March it was a case of tours of duty in the line and then behind in support positions.

As winter slowly and reluctantly permitted the green fingers of Spring to dress the land, he learned of the moves preparatory to the huge Spring Offensive. That it was to be the final battle of the campaign was evidenced by the increased aerial activity, the accumulation of large stocks of ammunition, reinforcements of both men and armoured vehicles, flame-throwing equipment and amphibious vehicles for river crossings. He had seen too many similar battle preparations to be mistaken in his belief. Confirmation came when his Division was warned to leave its mountain sector and move into its attack jumping-off positions near the bank of the River Senio to the south east of Bologna.

The Brigade to which he belonged was withdrawn from the line to rest and plan for its part in the attack. Local leave was granted and he immediately wrote to Nicola and gave her the probable date of his arrival in Florence and suggested a meeting place near the Ponte Vecchio, the only bridge spanning the River Arno, left comparatively untouched by the German Army in 1944, the previous year. The days before their reunion sped by, bringing with them three further loving letters from her. These he read over and over again before adding them to the neat bundle of her letters in his haversack.

They eventually met when the buds of spring were just breaking. Although he had thought often of the moment of their meeting, he found he was strangely unprepared when he first saw her waiting for him. For a moment her loveliness blinded him and she seemed to be even younger than he remembered, even though but three months had passed since their first meeting. She stood still, awaiting his approach, her soft hazel eyes wide beneath her delicately arched brows. Her parted lips were cold for but an instant before his own melted into them and she was, where she always belonged, within the secure strength of his arms. Oblivious to everyone and everything, they stood, hands linked, committing each other to shuttered memory; then came a fractional sliver of shyness between them as if to permit a re-avowal of their mutual love.

Dreamlike, they walked through the major streets and squares, simply happy in each others company. Great monuments, churches and public palaces conveyed a vivid sense of the past, but it was the present they shared most. Later, in the crowded, rattling bus they sat close and he smelt the beauty of her. Her brown curled hair intoxicated him with its myriad scents of fresh spring air and sunshine, the faint warm smell of her naturalness and even the well-remembered hints of Rome, their first meeting-place. She, in turn, buried herself in his rough masculine tenderness, showing her need of him in her every look and with soft-gestured possessiveness. Endlessly, he repeated within himself, 'God, how I love you, Nicola.'

He knew himself to be reasonably competent and decisive in battle situations, well able to lead his men by example and self-denial, but here, with Nicola, he was a man so much in love that he was prepared to indulge her every whim if only their joyful happiness might continue indefinitely. This, she knew by intuition, but was also aware of the quiet strength his protective love gave to her and accepted this as a gift bestowed upon her especially.

They alighted from the bus some distance from the small stone farmhouse in which they were to stay during his brief leave period. Shouldering his Army pack, he cradled Nicola with his other free arm and they walked along the track edged with the tender green blades of spring grasses and early flowers. Their pace was slow and deliberate as if they were determined to eke out their moments together. Nicola's relatives met them outside the farmhouse. Alberto, a tall, kindly man, whose hands bespoke a lifetime's work on the land and who had been a stalwart member of the local Partisan Group when the Germans occupied the area and then came his wife, Maria, a smile creasing her round nut-brown face; equally as hardworking as her husband. Their own children had grown up and had emigrated to America and he and Nicola found themselves accepted most readily as a part of a suddenly enlarged family. Nicola, who had arrived the previous day, led him to the small room provided for them. He noted her small suitcase on the bed, the toy cuddly rabbit with its one buttoned-eye look perched in the centre of the two pillows on the bed, and then saw a vase of small flowers on the top of the chest of drawers, their fresh colours reflecting narcissus-like in the polished surface of the wood. They exchanged amusing, caring glances simultaneously; their night together in Rome and her frequent references to their bedtime company - the rabbit - uppermost in their thoughts. He lowered his pack to the floor and slowly lifted her hands to his lips and pressed a kiss within each palm. Equally slowly and deliberately he replaced her arms by her sides.

Before the evening meal, they walked together in the surrounding countryside. With their arms linked they ambled along the lanes, talking and laughing the time away. Although utterly indifferent to time itself, they were captivated by their surroundings, the peace and tranquillity of which touched them mutually. He had realised that Italy in early Spring was beautiful, but never quite like this. In these parts the callous scars of war were not readily seen, possibly because of the rapidity of the German withdrawal, and, in any event, the main defence line lay further to the North beyond the high mountain ridges.

As the evening shadows lengthened and placed their coolness upon the land, they retraced their steps. For both of them it had been an idyllic interlude in which their love had been reaffirmed beyond all doubt.

CHAPTER SIX

Immediately after their meal, they were ushered off to their room, their offers to help in the domestic chores kindly, but firmly, rebuffed by Alberto and Maria. It was as if all present knew that each passing moment possessed its own precious charm and was vibrant with life and love. Nicola did not speak of the time when his short leave would end, nor of the last battle in which she knew he would be involved. It was enough simply to be with him and to know that she possessed his love entirely.

They lay close in the darkness of the room, her head upon his chest, his arms cradling her. Outside the un-curtained window, a light wind caressed the wooded hills and occasionally murmured against the window pane as if seeking entry. His finger tips brushed her bare rounded shoulders as they talked quietly.

'Carlo', she said, almost dreamingly, 'Do you think that love like ours is known to us in a moment?'

'Yes, I think I do,' he conceded, after a thoughtful pause. 'But what prompted you to ask?' he added, inquisitively.

'Well,' she replied, 'We met so briefly and yet we both knew, didn't we?'

'Nicola, my love, if something so important is not known to us in an instant, it will never be known in a lifetime.'

'But we recognised it so suddenly,' she persisted, gently.

'Perhaps it was natural affinity,' he replied, drawing her warm young body closer to him.

'What's affinity, Carlo?' she enquired, her small slender fingers tracing designs in the hollow of his neck.

He kissed her tenderly, before replying. 'I suppose,' he said, creasing his forehead as if to seek the apt reply, 'It is like seeking a treasure which only you know exists, but are unaware of what it looks like, and then actually finding it in a place where you least expect to find it.' His lips brushed her fluttering eyelids through which the faintest shadows of her eyes could be seen, 'Such as you, Nicola,' he said, finally. Her eyes opened and she looked up at him, 'I like that, Carlo', she said, smilingly, 'That's like poetry.'

'And so are you to me,' he replied, 'But you know that already, don't you?' he queried teasingly.

'Mmm,' she murmured archly, her soft hands exploring him. 'And I have affinity with you too' and guided his hands in confirmation. Suddenly, her coral lips blossomed against him and he knew a world of untold delight as if he were being taken through passages hung with burgundy red tapestry, carpeted with softest fur. New vistas constantly unfolded before him until fevered ardour gave way to an exquisite languor and they both slept. She curled delicately against him, lest in the fluid, jewelled darkness, he slip away.

Later, in the night, he fought himself to the surface of wakefulness from a hazy nightmare in which he had been intensely alone. He remembered becoming colder and colder as his searches failed to find Nicola and his vision of her fading dully the longer the searches went on. Dimly, above his head, he saw the ceiling, then his eye traversed the walls and, finally he saw her warm still body beside him - faint blue shadows beneath her eyes. He lay motionless beside her and then, suddenly, with a sigh of relief that the nightmare had gone and he had found her, he clasped her sleepy body and held her desperately; desire and fear within his heart. The night was thereafter timeless and they saw it merge slowly and beautifully into breaking day. Maria brought them coffee and remained for a short time sitting at the foot of the bed discussing with them plans for the remainder of their stay. He expressed the hope that he and Nicola might be allowed to help about the farm and in the vineyards, for he wished to repay the many kindnesses and human understanding extended to them.

Maria was delighted at the suggestion and avowed that before his leave finished, Alberto would make a farmer of him and that Nicola would become a farmer's wife. It was said with such light-heartedness that, when Maria left them, they laughed at the notion, but, nevertheless, were pleased at the prospect of helping. She cupped his stubbly chin and the lean sides of his face in her small warm hands and gazed seriously at him. Her hazel eyes were wide with concern and tenderness and he knew he could never envisage life without her. Later, like a small child, she watched him shave and seemed so interested that he was compelled to ask if she had seen such activity before.

'Not someone I love so much', she replied, bestowing a winsome smile upon him. She had told him previously of the loss of her parents during a bombing raid on Naples where they had once lived, and of the want and hardship, she and her aunt had subsequently endured. It had been intended as a prelude to her explanation of the style of her life she had followed before their meeting, but he had kissed her explanations away. He had not wished to know of the other soldiers who had entered her life - it was not important to him. That they had found each other gave life its true meaning for him. It was enough. Apart from the comradeship he shared with his Section, his life, too, had been comparatively empty and purposeless, before Nicola had entered it. He had always needed someone like her to provide his life with real meaning; to enable a natural expression of the love and affection within him and to return it in full. He finished shaving, dried his face and pulled her gently towards him. 'Do you know, young lady', he said with a soft smile about his lips, 'What Victor Hugo said about us?'

She shook her head negatively, querying the question with her eyes.

'He said that the supreme happiness in life is the conviction that we are loved.'

'Did he really say that?' she asked.

'Well, the saying is attributed to him and he was a great French writer, so I suppose he wrote it for a Nicola and a Charles who lived in France when he was alive.'

'I like him for that one saying alone,' she said, decidedly.

'Of course, he wrote many other things,' he explained.

'Have you read them, Carlo?'

'Not all of them - only *Notre Dame* and *Les Miserables*, but I hope to read his other books one day.'

'We'll read them together, Carlo? In our very own house one day when all work is done and the whole world and all time is ours.'

'I like you for that one saying alone,' he said, chidingly.

CHAPTER SEVEN

During the rest of the day he assisted Alberto whilst Nicola helped Maria. In the spring sunshine, he and Alberto worked hard and their conversation naturally turned to the bitter warfare being waged to the North. He learned that his companion had been a member of the Committee of National Liberation and had taken part in many Partisan battles against the Germans in and around Florence. Alberto told him of the reprisal action of the Germans in March of the previous year following a Partisan attack on a detachment of fifty soldiers from South Tyrol. The Germans had taken three hundred and thirty five hostages to the Ardeatina Tunnels, outside Rome, where the SS troops had shot them and then mined the tunnels to bury the bodies. Alberto told the story in a matter of fact tone, but there was no mistaking the hatred he felt for the German Troops concerned.

They spoke too, of the Italy of Dante and Michelangelo and of the First World War when Alberto fought high up in the cold passes of the Alps against the same enemy. Despite its misfortunes, Alberto obviously had a great love for his country and its music. In a rich baritone voice he would sing snatches from various Operas as they worked together.

The two remaining days of his leave saw them both working busily about their respective chores inside and outside the farm, but, each afternoon, with the tacit consent of Alberto and Maria -

their 'bosses' as they called them, feelingly - they wandered off into the adjacent countryside. Already the days were warmer and they soon found a space high on the hillside where, protected by the rocky outcrops, they would sit, talk and gaze at far off Florence, spread out before them. Nicola would indicate the Duoma, the medieval towers and endeavour to tell him a little about the Florentines of the Renaissance period. Her schooling had been as scanty as his own, but she became beautifully articulate when conjuring up for him the inhabitants of the Florentine yesterworld.

She told him of the Tuscan Spring following the damp bleak winter, and of the visitors, pilgrims, merchants and other travellers who, like tourists, would reach their peak at Easter time. She regaled him with a long cycle of the Religious Festivals and the numerous holy holidays of the patron saint of Florence, John the Baptists, whose feast day, began on the 24th June every year.

He listened attentively to all she told him, and wished all History could be made so real and true in descriptive terms.

'Perhaps,' he interjected, 'We might be here together on the 24th June, if the War is over by then.'

She caught his mood and excitedly said, 'And you might be stationed in Florence and we could come up here in the hills and have our very own "picnic-feast".'

'Wherever we are on that day,' he said seriously, 'I shall always be thinking of you and loving you, Nicola, so don't mind too much if our wish doesn't come true.'

She sensed his thoughts had gone from the present to the days yet to come before the War was over. She drew him close to her, pressed his head lightly against her breasts and caressed his cheek. 'Don't worry, Carlo, my love,' she said softly. 'I know in my heart that one day we shall be together for always.' She held him tightly as if to shut out all the intervening coldness and loneliness of the War and its demands upon them.

He turned upwards in her arms, bent her lips to his own and kissed her lightly. Thereafter they spoke no more of the time of his leaving.

On the morning of his last day with them, Alberto told him of the arrangements made for Nicola to stay at the farm until the spring battles were over when effective plans could be made for their marriage and future. He and Alberto were of similar mind and outlook both regarding work matters and Nicola's welfare, and he knew she would be well cared for in his absence.

The vague, tenuous future held no terrors for him, for he knew in his innermost being that his actions were morally correct and that all would be well in the end. That night, with her soft innocent face close to his own, he felt himself to have been charged with the safekeeping of a very precious person. All previous events in his life appeared to have been intended that he might all the more appreciate the priceless love given to him so warmly and openly by the young girl who lay quietly beside him. Her face was serene and tranquil in sleep, her slightly parted lips revealing her small, white teeth. He lay awake for a while guarding her against the night, his arm beneath her shoulders growing gradually numb even with her light weight upon it. He thought of their tender love-making before she slid away to sleep when her eyes brimmed with both softness and a form of wanton passion, as if she wanted their last night together to be inscribed permanently in their hearts and minds.

Before dawn, a deep contented sleep claimed him and he awoke to find that Nicola had quietly left him and prepared their light breakfast. She had also packed his few items of kit and personal effects in his army pack on top of which she had placed her small Saint Christopher Medallion on its thin filigree chain.

'But it's yours, Nicola,' he had protested, when endeavouring to return it to her. 'No, Carlo, it's ours and will bring you safely back to me,' she replied, with soft insistence.

They had discussed but briefly their respective religious views and beliefs and there was complete accord between them as to what constituted a good or bad life. As a young boy, he had had the teachings of the Church pumped into him, but had long ago learned for himself the true meaning of Christianity - it was not always to be found in churches or stately cathedrals. For him, it was to be found in the eyes and in the hearts of mankind itself and manifested itself quite clearly when encountered.

In the vicious artillery bombardments below the heights of Cassino he had prayed often into the earthen walls of his dugout as the violence shattered the world immediately about him. Such prayers as he made now were always for the wellbeing of Nicola and a continuance of their mutual love. He asked for no more than that, and the more tangible, material things, did not interest him. He was certain that he would eventually find work of a suitable nature and with sufficient re-numeration to enable him and Nicola to lead a useful life together. Perhaps, even, he mused, they might one day have a family and imagined most vividly a daughter as loveable and warm-hearted as Nicola herself. He smiled inwardly at the pleasing prospect, but that was for the future to decide. At present, there was the moment of farewell to consider - a thought he had purposely deferred ever since their meeting in Florence only a few days before.

He was aware that Nicola would show distress at his leaving, but it was shared in an equal degree by Alberto and Maria. Both hugged him close and kissed his cheeks in the true warm-hearted manner that Italians had with close friends.

'You have always a home here with us, Carlo', Alberto said feelingly, and then added, almost gruffly, 'Don't forget us, Amico.'

'I'll never do that,' he replied, grasping Alberto's huge extended hand.

Nicola had his pack ready, but before leaving, he took Maria's hands within his own and kissed them lightly. He raised his eyes to hers, bent forward and then kissed her cheeks. 'Goodbye, Maria', he said gently. 'Take care of Nicola for me.' Maria nodded dumbly and went to Alberto and clasped him protectively.

He turned away from them and saw Nicola, a sad, brave half-smile on her small face, ready to accompany him to the path leading to the distant roadway. His parting wave to Alberto and Maria returned and with Nicola at his side, he walked towards the road where he knew he would be able to obtain a lift on a passing military vehicle into Florence. Before reaching the road edge, he stopped and drew Nicola tenderly and finally towards him. 'Goodbye, my only love,' he almost whispered. Her lips sought his and she held him close until he felt her warm tears seal their farewell kiss - this saltiness a part of her inner self being entrusted to his care.

He withdrew slowly from her embrace and walked away. At the road verge, he glanced back, acknowledged her final wave, and then set out in the direction of Florence.

PART TWO

DEATH

CHAPTER EIGHT

His pace responded to his subdued mood. His boots on the metalled road surface beat out his thoughts. 'I love you, Nicola, I love you', they echoed repeatedly. He looked back but a curve in the road concealed the farm and the small track where he had left his reason for living. Again, he entertained the same thought as he did when they parted in Rome, but a strong sense of duty prevented him from flying back to her. The sound of a truck behind him caught up with his thoughts and quickly he flagged down the driver and co-driver and obtained a lift in the vehicle. Flinging his pack over the tailboard, he clambered aboard and made himself secure on one of a number of wooden crates forming the vehicle's load.

He was oblivious to the passing scenery and let his thoughts travel down the paths of memory; of the days and nights with Nicola. Her image was ever before him and his heart went out to her for the tears she had shed for him. No one ever before had provided him with such unselfish love and sweet-scented warmth.

On arriving in Florence, he was singularly fortunate in securing further transport and, towards late afternoon, he alighted, somewhat stiffly, from a jeep in which he had been taken to the Headquarters of his Brigade. Then followed the assembly of all leave personnel and within an hour he was again with his Section. During the evening meal, they all discussed their various adventures and events during their brief leave period, but he kept his innermost thoughts locked within him when taking part in the discussion.

Three days of preparation, various inspections and explanations of the plans for the coming offensive followed, before his platoon left its rest area and, in a motorised convoy drove over the spine-ridged Appenines and entered Forli, a small town on the highway leading from Rimini through Bologna to Milan.

At first, he found the flat farmlands, banked rivers and the Adriatic Sea bordering the front line, very strange and oddly peaceful after the mountainous confines. Everywhere he saw the metalled sinews of modern war. Artillery, battery upon battery in sand-bagged pits covered with blotched camouflage netting. Tanks, with lethally pointed 75mm guns, muzzles covered, squatting, squadron after squadron, beneath the trees. As they approached the front line beyond the flat skyline, he saw the usual shell craters mostly full of black, still water because of the low-lying land. On the rear of a floodbank of the River Senio, he and his section dug their trenches, put out barbed wire and a few protective anti-personnel mines. At intervals on the wire they hung old cans on a trip wire to ensure they had advance warning of approaching enemy patrols. Their activity was shielded by an artillery programme of harassing fire on the German troops dug in on the other side of the river. Smoke shells dropped regularly with the high explosive shells and the usual acrid, bitter smell assailed his nostrils. How he loathed and detested the stench and smell of war and longed for the softness and warmth of Nicola and the sweet scent of her presence. She had added a new dimension to his world and had sharpened his natural soldierly self-preservation instincts, for, as the evening ribbons of half light stretched into darkness, flashes in the northern sky triggered his senses. Quickly he ensured his men were in their dug outs under cover and, within seconds, a heavy German artillery bombardment began. The shells thudded thickly into the ground around them. Huge fountains of earth and smoke towered up as the vile coughing of the soft water-inundated earth began. Upheavals of sound and colour, black, yellow, orange bursts of fury and torn mud. Blasted earth was re-blasted within seconds as the shells followed each other, each seeming to vie with its forerunner in maliciousness and destruction. Saliva drooled down the side of his mouth as sickness gripped his bowels. Yet again, it was for him the moment of truth and the realisation of his mere mortality. He fought within himself to regain composure, licked his lips dry and gave a crooked grin to one of the younger members of his section.

'Only evening hate, young Ollie', he said laconically. 'They do it to catch the ration parties coming up after dark.'

'Does it last long, Corp?' the lad enquired, nervously, his eyes wide in a white drawn face beneath his steel helmet.

'Not usually, they haven't got many shells left over there. They've nearly had it,' he replied deliberately, with the intention of instilling confidence in the lad. Dusty Miller, another member of the section, who had seen his fair share of action, broke into the conversation, 'Yeah, they're getting rid of them to save lugging them back to Germany'. The newcomer brightened at the interjection, but Easton knew that there would be many more such bombardments to be endured before the final victory was won.

He felt concern for his section of 15 men and knew what fatal results could be induced through an over-imaginative assessment. However, it was his job to nurse the newcomers through the first difficult stages and, if they lived, they themselves would soon become seasoned campaigners. The shelling ceased abruptly and he used the breathing space to check that no casualties had been incurred before attending to his own welfare.

Spreading his groundsheet three-quarters over the top of his dug out, he earthed down the sheet edges and dug a small drainage channel on each side with a downhill directional flow. It was an old infantryman's dodge to drain off rain water or heavy dew in the night. He looked out into the darkness, pleased with the news he had received earlier from his Platoon Commander that another Company was providing standing patrols during the night. They, themselves, would be on such patrols soon enough.

He never truly slept when in the Line; the responsibility for his men precluded it. Inevitably it was a case of fitful dozes from time to time, then out to check that lookouts were awake and at their posts. A cigarette craftily cupped in hand, shared with a young lookout - a wisecrack or two, reassurance, brief talk of home and family, leave spells, after the war hopes and ambitions. Such confidence he gave to his men often left him drained, but now, with Nicola in his life, he found he had more to give of a source of confidence that had but been awakened. He longed to survive the coming battle for her sake, but he was resolved that it would not be at the expense of his men to whom he owed so much.

CHAPTER NINE

The previous rumours of the big attack proved correct when, in the first clean heart-lifting days of April, amphibious crab-like vehicles crawled up close behind the front line. The weather remained clement and the torn shell-pocked trees in a nearby farm pushed forth faint spindly leaves of greenness. What he thought were swallows, curved through the gun-flecked evening sky, and in the grasses and reeds of the river bank, nature's industrious citizens went about their affairs. Battalion Orders were issued, Company Commanders held their conferences and, finally, his Platoon Commander briefed him and the other Non-Commissioned Officers on the plan of attack and objectives to be taken.

His Platoon Commander, a likeable, uncomplicated man, courageous to a fault but a comparative newcomer, having been seconded from a Heavy Anti-Aircraft Battery of the Royal Artillery, gave them the Divisional Commander's plan of attack. Zero hour would be just before dawn when a heavy barrage would be laid down on the German gun and mortar positions and the front line trenches. Flame-throwing vehicles would lead the infantry carrying vehicles which would then cross the river barrier. The attacking troops would be boxed within a creeping barrage with Royal Artillery Officers and Royal Air Force Liaison Officers well to the fore. RAF Tyhoon fighter planes would bomb and strafe the enemy immediately ahead to keep them engaged as the first wave of attackers crossed the river. The momentum of the assault was to continue non-stop; fresh divisions would leap-frog each other maintaining the attack that would go by both night and day. The American Divisions of the 5th Army would also attack in the mountainous area to their left flank to give the Germans little opportunity to switch troops to the threatened fronts.

He passed on the orders to his section, arranged for them to get as much rest as possible before dawn the next day, and checked rations, water, first-aid field kits and that all weapons were serviceable. The waiting hours passed slowly and towards dawn, when birds and all living things were hushed, the darkness yielded to the first groping fingers of the coming day. Suddenly there was a shrill singing in the air, the light was broken by the ragged flashes of guns firing from the rear, their shells rending and tearing the air as they stabbed their hateful passage to the enemy lines. Sudden blossomings of yellow, black, orange and green erupted as they seeded the earth making man's inhumanity to man grotesquely manifest. Shell after shell fell to shake the bowels of the earth and earth, light and sound become inextricably mixed. Rivulets of earth fell down the quaking sides of his dug out as the ground rumbled and shook with hatred and fear. Shells drummed and drilled into the enemy positions, but gradually the German counter-battery fire began to take its human toll. Cries for stretcher bearers became more frequent and he was relieved when the verbal order for the attack was given.

Clambering ungainly out of their dug outs he and his men moved forward in their set formation with about four yards between each man. Laden down with their weapons and equipment they entered the hellish inferno of dirt, dust and the demented sound of the cross barrages. The fresh smell of living things was everywhere. Overhead, but unseen, they heard the Tyhoon planes boring in, lethally low and then heard the sharp explosions of bombs and rockets discharged over the German front line. Placing himself centrally, he led his section up the floodbank keeping to the tape-marked paths through the minefields, partially marked by the Divisional Engineers.

Coloured rockets soared from the German Infantry posts signalling to their own artillery for assistance to repel the attack, but to no avail. The offensive gradually gathered strength and could not be halted, however much the German guns were able to reply. Already the water-borne troops were being ferried across the river. The troop carriers lurched ungainly up the opposing bank, nosed through shell-blasted gaps in the wire, shook the water from their undercarriage and waddled irresistibly ever forward. Small groups of German prisoners, grey-faced, dirty and dust-covered, filtered wearily back to the rear areas. Some, badly wounded, were helped by their comrades walking slowly and considerately - others, still in death, lay in their gun positions. Everywhere lay the horrible, wasted litter of the battlefield. Helmets, wrecked guns, weapons, letters, ugly rust-brown stained field dressings, clothing, shell and bullet cases. Fire and smoke engulfed the entire area - tongues of flame from wrecked tanks and vehicles. The smoke obscured even the daylight itself.

Breathing became difficult as they groped blindly forward and he was relieved when it became the turn of his Section to be ferried across the seething river, its surface whipped and lashed by invisible machine gun fire from the German second defence lines. He took the opportunity in the carrier to check on his men and found no casualties had been incurred. Each earthen covered face, smoke blackened rivulets of sweat etched into it. Knowing that it was but the beginning of a hard fight to clear the Germans from their defence lines, he displayed, as far as he was able, a confident air that infected his men. Cigarettes were distributed, grumbles aired, jokes exchanged wryly and morale boosted.

Suddenly, as the carrier mounted the far bank, a searing explosion shook its tracks and the vehicle reared up, its front clawing the sky like a terrified horse he had once seen being ill-treated. He heard the mine fragments hit and shatter the thin protective plates, saw the foul spumes of dirt and grey black smoke and heard the cries and moans of those of his men wounded by the lethal shards of steel. Apart from a dull headache and a feeling of light-headedness he had, as far as he could gather, escaped injury. Quickly he helped other survivors of the mine blast to free the wounded whose gaunt and bloodless faces showed the severity of their wounds. Without pausing, his head aching from the blast, his vision blurred, he tirelessly dressed the wounds of his companions, lit cigarettes for the less severely wounded and sent a runner to the rear for medical assistance.

CHAPTER TEN

The murderous machine gun fire slackened and the sound of the barrage rumbled away in the distance - obvious signs that the attack had been successful. On the arrival of the stretcher bearers and medical personnel, he reassured those of his men who remained alive and unwounded and led them forward once again to the attack. A huge dust cloud hung over the battlefield blotting out the daylight. He felt himself to be in an unknown world with unseen death and destruction on every side. Sounds were intense and unreal at the same time, and almost trance-like, he and his section trod the torn earth going ever forward to the still shell-shocked, red-rimmed horizon.

Towards noon, he met up with the rest of his Platoon, reported to the Commander and, after a hurried meal break, the advance was resumed. Throughout the long afternoon, strongpoints were overcome, their defenders forced out by bomb and bayonet but not without cost. From time to time high explosive shells with hideous black air bursts fell away among the thin line of attacking troops.

He and his few remaining men were by now almost exhausted, and it was time for the reserve division to take over the momentum of the attack to exploit the breakthrough. Wearily he stumbled ahead of his Section, his senses still alert despite his tiredness and throbbing temples. They had almost reached the

German third defence line when beneath his feet he heard the deadly unmistakeable click of compression of a German Schu mine. He had seen many such anti-personnel mines detonated by unsuspecting infantry and knew the hideous wounds they inflicted on the human body from the waist downwards. Shouting at his men to remain where they were, he tried to control his trembling limbs. He knew that as long as he kept the mine mechanism compressed with his body weight, the mine would not throw its explosive charge above the surface and detonate viciously.

For what seemed an eternity he stood stock still as his mind wrestled with the problem of what action he should take. Ideas raced each other in his mind, each as useless as the one preceding it. He knew that his only salvation lay in his split second reaction, once he had removed his boot compressing the three prongs of the mine. With his other boot he awkwardly scraped a channel about four feet in length in the torn and trampled earth beside him. The deeper he could make it the greater his chances of survival, that he knew for certain. He refused to let him men assist him as there was always a cluster of such mines sown, never a single one.

From the distance they watched his despairing, desperate efforts, longing to help but were fully aware that their approach would surely detonate further mines. His legs ached and grew more visibly weary as the sweat dropped from him. He rested, regained a little of his strength and, with a convulsive jerking motion, lifted his foot and threw himself prone and sideways into the shallow excavation. The mine burst cruelly above the earth and lashed the air with its vile explosion. He felt the heat of its detonation, heard the shrill whine of its steel pellets in the air above him and sank unconscious into a morass of blood-red darkness.

Remote from his body, his mind remained suspended in a tightly wrapped cocoon of pain and darkness. He was momentarily outside of life itself and yet saw himself dragged out of the shallow grave by two of his Section after three others had been killed in their attempts to pull him from the minefield. He heard dully the explosions that took their lives yet could do nothing to save them. Most disturbing of all, he found he did not recognise them nor could he rationalise his thought processes. Through the fog of pain he tried to speak but found his vocal chords muffled as strange sounds fought their way for utterance. Long, dark hours followed made up of jolting movement and ever-consuming pain. Then a sudden peace after a further small injection of pain. He longed to be safe and had an anguished need for some particular person to comfort him but did not know who it was he was seeking. The name he sought in his mind forever eluded him, the face he tried to conjure up dissolved before his attempts at identification. He lived in one long nightmare of uncertainty, of never-ending corridors down which his poor, suffering shell-shocked thoughts raced in search of an essential part of his life, but never finding it.

PART THREE

RESURRECTION

CHAPTER ELEVEN

The coin he had once thrown in the Treviso Fountain brought him back to Rome in a hospital train, gently jolting through the night hours. But he neither knew it nor realised that the person he sought with all his heart and broken mind sat forlornly in the small flat but a short distance away. The cold, grey platform where they first met, slowly but surely receded into the distance as the train imperceptibly gathered speed.

Occasionally his mind verged on the borders of consciousness and he tried desperately to unscramble his ravelled thoughts. Something remained concealed and he fought to find it but in vain. After a brief stay in a Base Hospital, where the minor gun shot lacerations to his body healed, he was flown back to England where he was admitted to a Military Hospital located in the South of Hampshire. The pleasant warm days passed slowly for him, but the anguish he felt within him was ever present. Gradually, his powers of speech returned and he spent many sessions with a visiting doctor who specialised in neurology. He was always addressed by rank and name, but they were strange words to him. At night in the ward he repeated them over and over again, hoping they might unlock the gates of memory. The months passed and his visitors, few in number, dressed awkwardly in new civilian clothes, tried to get him to recognise them as members of his depleted Section. They left, their efforts unsuccessful, helpless pity in their eyes.

In his empty, lonely purblind world, he found himself turning to nature as a means of relating himself to life that went on relentlessly. In the hedgerows, delicately he fingered aside the young green leaves to see the Spring homes of the sparrows and the finches. Ribbons of green pastureland rising to the low hills were for him a source of constant delight. He leaned against the rough, gnarled trees in the spinney and forests and watched intently almost wistfully, the hesitant hoppity rabbits come out towards sunset in search of food. He stood as still as the trees themselves and like each of them he was alone - yet envied the mingling of their leaves rustling high overhead. He grew rugged and strong as a result of the semi-outdoor life he led, but each morning and evening there was the loneliness of the hospital ward to be faced.

It was during one of his country walks that he found he was in a quiet country lane that led him to a farm tucked below softly protective hills. Hay-making had been in progress and he watched interestedly as the tractors deliberately circled at the end of each swathing run. He visited frequently and the genial farmer who owned the land let him assist in various ways about the farm. Vaguely, he knew that he had done such work before - somewhere, sometime - and that it had special and pleasurable associations for him. It was but a tenuous link with his past, but he held on to it resolutely in his mind. He now knew his own name and that he had once worked on a farm - there would be further links in the days ahead if he fought hard enough to regain his memory.

The months of summer and autumn passed and he obtained a job with the farmer who, unknown to him, had been approached by the medical authorities at the hospital who realised the beneficial effects of outdoor work for their patient. Shortly afterwards, he received his discharge from the Army and was awarded a disablement pension which, although sufficient for his immediate needs, required the augmentation of his weekly salary at the farm to enable him to negotiate the purchase of a small cottage nearby. Although his shell-shocked condition had improved noticeably, the events in his life prior to his admission to hospital remained for him a completely blank page.

CHAPTER TWELVE

One day, when the first of the winter winds sythed the last of the russet leaves of autumn from the trees, he was sitting outside one of the barns in the bleak, watery sunshine. It was his mid-day meal break and, as he idly tossed breadcrumbs from his meal to the inquisitive but strangely timorous sparrows, his employer, accompanied by a stranger, a tall burly man, interrupted his meal.

The man was introduced to him as a Mr Logan, who possessed information regarding a former friend whom he had known in the past. His employer left them after giving him to understand that there was no need for his return to work during the afternoon. He took an instant liking to the stranger and, anxious though he was to learn of the reason for his visit, took him to his cottage before broaching the subject. Settled in old, but comfortable, armchairs in the low-ceilinged sitting room, they talked. The man opened their conversation by producing a photograph of a young girl and asked him if he recognised her. For an instant only his mind seemed to make a fractional recognition, but then the moment was gone and he had to acknowledge truthfully that he did not know the person depicted. He was asked if her name, Nicola, had any associations for him, and again, after the merest flicker of doubt he gave a negative reply. That he was intrigued was obvious and his questioner patiently explained that he was a Private Investigator acting on behalf of the young girl concerned who had made several enquiries to locate him. She was unable to visit the country herself and was still in Rome but had regularly forwarded money to facilitate the enquiries she wished to be made. Further talk followed but the discussion of the past and his former association with the girl jogged no chord of memory. Before leaving, his companion gave him the photograph and an address in Rome where the girl could be located and, finally, his own official card. After the man had gone, he looked t the card more closely and read, 'Christopher Logan', Private Investigator, 39 Wigmore Street, London WI. Telephone Welbeck 4774. Nervously he turned the card repeatedly between his fingers. Something stirred in his mind, but it was not the man's calling, the address or the telephone number, more the card itself. Suddenly he realised that it was the Christian name that had for him the faintest of recollections. He had known someone or something of that name in the past. During the night he lay awake trying to recall who or what it was and frequently looked at the photograph by the aid of his bedside lamp. The soft, tender look in her eyes had been captured to perfection by the photographer and he longed with all his soul to understand how she had belonged in his past life. He thought that perhaps a visit to Rome during his annual holiday due in the early part of the following year might enable him to regain his lost memories, and resolved to make the necessary arrangements without delay.

The cold, slow winter days followed one by one and now that the main farming work was over, he found himself with more time for leisure pursuits. He explored on foot all the surrounding countryside and one Sunday morning he heard the toll of church bells rolling towards him through the leafless trees. Drawn by their sound he found the entrance to a small stone church and, without really knowing why, joined the parry of church-goers as they entered the church porch. Inside, quiet organ music blended with the now muted peal of bells. He seated himself on a rose-coloured pew just inside the entrance and a peacefulness came upon him. The bells and music ceased and the morning service began.

Whenever the rest of the congregation knelt or rose he did likewise, but he was always wide-eyed and watchful during the moments of prayer. His visit to the church was, he thought, for some mysterious purpose and he was ever-vigilant to discover it. He studied closely the tall, thin vicar whose kindly face was matched by an equally pleasant speaking voice. In turn, he looked at each member of the congregation but his inspection prompted no element of recognition. A hush descended as the young vicar climbed the few stairs to the pulpit. He watched the slender sensitive fingers open the Bible with practiced skill and heard the modulated voice announce that the text for the sermon was taken from the 11th Chapter of the Epistle according to Saint John in the New Testament. He listened at first with polite interest until the vicar referred to the waking of Lazarus and that when he heard of the circumstances of the death, Jesus wept. As if from a distance, he heard the vicar's voice continue and talk of the resurrection of the life of Lazarus. But the words that he heard stirred some small part of his memory, 'Jesus wept' ran continually through his brain. That they possessed a significance for him he knew, but the link would not fall into place. Leaving the church at the end of the service, he absentmindedly shook the vicar's hand and walked quickly away, his thoughts churning endlessly over the words that he had heard. He felt as if he were nearing a gate of hope and realisation of a secret unknown longing. As he walked back to his cottage, he pondered on the things that he knew were important to him in his search to restore his shattered memory. Rabbits he had seen at sunset, the farm, Christopher Logan - there must be something else to close the chain and he thought hard and long on what it might be or what form it might take. Wakeful nights with their solemn paced hours of darkness became second nature to him and he grew thin of feature. Although he worked as hard as ever, labour appeared to be a kind of anodyne, as if it would tire him so physically that his miserable tortured mind might then find rest.

As Christmas approached, his appearance caused his employer's wife reason for concern, and she reacted by inviting him to the farm on Christmas Eve, when a small party for the farm workers was to take place. Appreciating her kindness, he accepted the invitation although he would have preferred the quietness of his own cottage. Contrary to his expectations, he enjoyed the warmth and companionship of those who attended and, when the party ended, he helped his hostess clear the tables. Whilst moving a half empty wine bottle from the kitchen sideboard she dropped the bottle on the stone floor. The shattering of the glass particles as the bottle smashed to the floor awoke a memory deep within him. He watched its red contents spread across the floor and knelt immediately to assist her gather the fragments of broken glass. As he did so he noticed the creased label adhering to one of the larger fragments. Carefully, almost tenderly, he picked it up and read 'Lachryma Christi' and in a blinding instant of eternal time he knew it to be the Italian for 'the tear of Christ'. Almost feverishly, he laced together the pieces of his broken memory. Like pearls strung on a gossamer thread, he related a rabbit toy with a Christopher medallion. He stood, white-faced, breathing deeply, willing his mind to respond to the promptings of his very soul. An interminable pause, then a farm with grapes and sunshine, love and warmth of belonging. Then, finally, a cascade of golden memory overwhelmed him and his tears fell unchecked and unashamedly when the lovely child-like face of Nicola came to him clearly from the wreaths of forgetfulness and tortured longing.

CHAPTER THIRTEEN

The same chilly wind of January now over a year old, sent its exploratory fingers along the cold snow-covered platform of Rome railway station as the train bearing Charles Easton slowly drew to a halt. He had written to Nicola of his probable time of arrival and, long before the train stopped, he had moved down its corridors to the place opposite the platform where he knew she would be waiting. The snow fell steadily from the dark sky and emphasised the vaulted arches of the station itself. His pulses beat feverishly and he was half sick with fear lest she was not there and that something dire had happened to her. His anxiety increased moment by moment until he finally beheld her small figure in the distance. As the trained neared her he saw her wearing the same fur coat she once wore long, long ago. She stood in the soft feathery snow, her young thin face wearing a smile of welcome and such delight that he leapt from the still slow-moving train. Slamming the carriage door behind him he ran along the platform towards her.

With the coat flared wing-like behind her, she ran into his outstretched arms, her beauty was ever fresh for him and he felt a wild joy surge within him. Their hearts and bodies met as his lips sought hers and, as the soft snow flakes fell wetly, he knew that never again would there be a parting between them. And, possibly, high above in the winter sky, in a place where peace is alleged to pass all understanding, there may well have been a person called Jesus who wept for them and their future happiness.

THE END

DAS BILD (THE PHOTOGRAPH)

For almost twenty-three years, Martin Hansen had kept the photograph, his reason for doing so becoming clearer to him as time went by. On many occasions he had vowed that he would one day make enquiries as to the identities of the soldier and his family, whom he presumed to be wife and daughter, depicted in the photograph, but had never taken positive action since he was convinced he had been responsible for the death of the soldier concerned.

Now, however, his resolve could become a possibility. He had that morning received a letter from his solicitor informing him of a substantial legacy left to him by an Aunt who had recently died. He had met his aunt but infrequently and had never been aware that any close bond existed between them. However, her generosity precluded further prevarication on his part regarding his quest.

He reflected on his course of action. First to ascertain the unit or regiment to which the dead man belonged and next to make enquiries of former comrades or friends to establish his name and his place of residence. Perhaps the insertion of advertisements in newspapers in the locality once it was established, might be of help. Also ex-servicemen journals or magazines might offer a useful line of enquiry. Next he thought of the dead man's family - the wife might not still be living, or, if she were, might have remarried, consequently these changes of name might hinder his search. He realized that all possibilities existed since he had left his decision so late. So allowances had to be made and he would tackle first things first.

In furtherance of this reasoning, he closely examined the photograph which he removed from his wallet. It measured five inches by three inches and three of its corners were missing. Its edges and surface were cracked and the print had a yellowish, almost decaying, tint. It was a balanced pose with the three figures centrally placed. The man was wearing the uniform of a private soldier and a forage cap with some form of Army insignia at its front. The man had a fresh, clean appearance, no doubt heightened by his close-cropped hair style. His right hand clasped the small trusting fingers of a girl, aged about 8 years, dressed in a short-sleeved cotton dress with a sash around the waist. Her fair and curly hair was bound with bows at either side above the ears, and a half-smile on her face showed the obvious pride in her father whose hand she clasped. To the child's left stood her mother in casual pose. She, too, wore a short-sleeved printed cotton dress, with stockings and open type sandal shoes. Her hair was dark and wavy and she was sturdily built even though she was at least a foot shorter than her husband. Her tanned face suggested she was of the country rather than town bred. Indeed, the background to the three figures showed a grass path bordering a small stream with several chickens on the far bank. The trees depicted were mainly coniferous and the snap appeared to have been taken in early summer. He turned the photograph over and saw, in his own handwriting... 'Taken from a dead soldier at Homs, Tripolitania, January 20th 1943'.

The occasion on which he had written the words he did not recall but knew it could not have been very long after he had buried the soldier concerned. The scene came back to him, not so readily or clear-cut nowadays, but fairly detailed, nevertheless. The night previously he had carried his machine-gun along a winding track to the right of the Homs-Miserata road, just outside Tripoli. For most of that night the advanced armoured contingent and the Infantry Regiment to which he belonged had endeavoured to hold an attack by the opposing infantry.

The enemy had not been dislodged and, following a change of plan, he and his gun team had climbed to the summit of a rocky outcrop where, just as the first streaks of dawn lightened the night sky, he brought his gun into action again. He found he was overlooking the flank of the advancing enemy infantry. He opened fire, switching from target to target and saw the troops fall as the belt of fire covered them. He was not, by nature, an aggressive person and throughout the various actions in the Western Desert had experienced his full share of fear and trepidation. It was the sight of the small groups of dead infantry from his regiment lying in front of the enemy positions that incensed him and made him uncaring on this particular morning. Belt after belt of ammunition was fed into the gun and immediately beneath its muzzle the earth was scorched with the rate of fire he had maintained despite the stoppages he had quickly rectified. Suddenly, the battle area quietened as the attacking infantry began to scramble from their positions to avoid his line of fire. Although it was never a clear-cut victory, it was evident that the enemy would pause before continuing the attack.

A sense of weariness overcame him and he numbly obeyed the order to cease fire and to dismantle the gun. He heard vaguely his Company Commander pass on the thanks of the Commanding Officer of the infantry for the close, accurate supporting fire given to his men. He descended the hill, removed the cordite deposits from the gun and thought of a meal. It was already late morning and from the insulated food containers sent up from his Company Headquarters, he and his gun team breakfasted on hard bread and hot coffee. He had little appetite and smoked a cigarette as he drank his coffee. Looking about him he saw the lines of tanks and vehicles on the road ready to depart in the direction of Tripoli. Burnt wrecks of tanks and trucks had been pushed from the road and only scorched marks on its surface bore witness to the severity of the action fought.

1t was then he had noticed the dead enemy soldier lying a short distance from the edge of the road. The thin drab uniform was torn in several places and the blood from the gun shot wounds had caked black around each laceration. The face was white, its features calm and silent; death had come instantly and a rifle was still clutched in the lifeless hands. Other dead were much in evidence, but not in his immediate vicinity, and Hansen felt uneasy in the presence of this particular body.

The sun had climbed higher in the cloudless sky, and he felt its heat through his tunic. With the increased warmth and stillness, masses of black flies had started to crawl heavily over the face of the dead man. It was the time during the aftermath of a battle, when rage subsides and those actually fighting become momentarily vulnerable. Sick inwardly at the carnage and yet pleased to be still alive, and well aware that other battles had to be endured, he never liked this moment.

Although he knew that the Graves Commission personnel would eventually reach the battlefield and bury the dead, he had a sudden desire to atone for his part in causing this man's death by burying him quietly and decently away from the sun's glare and quick decomposition. Perhaps a peaceful spot, where neither flies nor the sounds of further battle would trouble him.

Acting on his resolve, with a spade taken from his equipment, he dug a shallow grave. Removing the identification tags and personal papers from the body, he rolled it gently into the grave and covered it as soundly as possible with earth. He placed the man's rifle with the helmet draped over it at the head of the grave and then glanced at the papers he had removed. Not wishing to know the name of the man he presumed he had killed, he did not read the particulars in the identity documents, but did extract the photograph from between its pages.

1t was the simplicity of the face of the child depicted that intrigued him to place the photograph in his tunic pocket. He then gave the other documents to his section commander and received mild censure for his actions. Nearly three months later, during another battle at the Mareth Line in Tunisia, he was wounded. Sent to a Base Hospital, he took no further part in the North African campaign.

Now, twenty-three years later, at the age of forty-two, he intended to find, if possible, the family of the dead soldier and assist them in any way he could. He readily conceded that curiosity as to the kind of family they were played an important part as to his motive. Also pleasing, was the prospect of travelling abroad again and the fact that his passport requirements were quickly dealt with. The following morning he wrote to the War Graves Commission for assistance in locating the official war cemetery in which the soldier had been eventually buried. A few days later the Commission replied that the former enemy country had moved many of their dead to cemeteries in Libya, but provided the names and particulars of ten former soldiers whose bodies had been recovered from the battlefield in question. Exact details of the next of kin were not immediately available, but further searches in records could be made if desired.

Encouraged by this prompt reply, he crossed the English Channel the next day, visited the Commission's premises, where having explained the reason for his enquiries, he was given the names and addresses of the nearest next of kin of the ten soldiers concerned. Having secured accommodation at a modest hotel, he travelled by road and rail during the next six weeks visiting nine of the ten addresses. His enquiries were thorough but the end of the period saw him no further forward in his search. However, he ruefully admitted that his command of the language had improved and that he liked the country.

Somewhat tired and dispirited even though it was midsummer and the weather was superb, he set out in a hired car, to visit the last address of those given to him. Its location was deep in the countryside close to the edge of a slow-running river. His enquiries disclosed that the cottage he sought was situated on the outskirts of a small village surrounded by woodland. The village had two hotels and in one he found accommodation. It was late afternoon and, after a meal, he rested and decided to leave his final search until the next day.

The next afternoon, feeling confident that his search would have a successful outcome, he drove to the outskirts of the village. The cottage had trees bordering it and their heavy branches shaded it from the sun's glare. He edged the car off the road into a dusty grey track, parking it close to a hedgerow. Keeping to the edge of the wood, he walked slowly towards the cottage, thinking of the manner he would broach the subject of his unannounced visit.

His approach was seen by a young girl about 8 years of age, standing on an upturned bucket in the rear garden, pegging out clothes on a line running from one of the corner eaves of the cottage to a low branch of a fruit tree in the far corner of the garden. Her fair hair tumbled about her shoulders as she stretched on tiptoe to peg the last of what appeared to be doll's clothes to the line. She smiled, as if she had been expecting him, and her light blue eyes sparkled in the sunshine. His intention had been to go to the front door of the cottage, but the girl invited him to enter the garden through a side gate.

'Have you come to see mummy? She's upstairs,' she said.

He was about to reply to her easy acceptance of him when, from an upstairs window, he heard a woman's voice call, 'Kathi, where are you? Come inside quickly.'

'Your mother?' he queried.

'Yes, she wants me - would you like to come and meet her?' the girl asked innocently.

'Yes, I'd like that very much, but I'll wait here, in the meantime.'

He heard her confide excitedly to her mother as she entered the cottage, and the whispered enquiry as to the visitor and the reason for his visit. He anticipated the child's negative reply by taking a further interest in the bright colourful confusion of the flower beds bordering the small garden lawn.

On hearing their approaching footsteps, he turned, bowing slightly, as they met.

'This is the gentleman, mummy,' the girl said, introducing him.

He clasped the extended hand of the mother and said immediately, 'My name is Martin Hansen. Please forgive me for calling unannounced.'

'Yes, it is a surprise,' she answered and continued, 'Would you care to come into the cottage?'

He did so and seated himself where shown on a low chintz covered settee in the pleasantly furnished sitting room. He looked at the girl's mother before continuing. She was, as he expected, about 30 years of age with the face of the young girl in the photograph still much in evidence. She was slightly over five feet tall and finely built. She wore a plain skirt and a white cotton blouse, the silver buttons on which sparkled in the sunshine filling the room. Her eyes, like her daughter's, were light blue and her hair almost a wheat coloured fairness. The features were fine and even, with the briefest of smiles at the corners of her small, full lips. Her manner, both courteous and pleasant, seemed to indicate that although she had known difficult times, she was of a good nature and kindly disposition. He knew instinctively that she would make it all the easier for him to explain his presence if it were in her power to do so. Thus reassured, he continued.

'I am right in assuming that you are Mrs Karen Meyer, and that before, your former surname was Frank?'

'Yes,' she replied quietly, 'I am still called Mrs Meyer.'

His previous enquiries had disclosed that her husband had died several years before when her daughter was very young, thus he understood her qualified reply.

'Mrs Meyer,' he began hesitantly, 'You may think it rather foolish of me to have come here today, but the truth is, I believe I once met your father many years ago in the Libyan Desert. That is', he said quickly, 'if he were a soldier serving in North Africa?'

His enquiries had been as detailed as possible and he was certain that her answer would confirm them, but it did not.

'No, Mr Hansen', she replied. 'My father died in the East in 1941 when I was about 7 years old, so it would appear that I am not the person you are seeking.'

Although momentarily nonplussed by her reply, her likeness to the girl in the photograph was beyond doubt and he felt certain he was not mistaken in his belief. He remained silent meeting her gaze and then removed the photograph from his wallet. He passed it to her and gently said 'But, surely, Mrs Meyer, this is a photograph of you as a young girl with your parents?'

She looked at the picture intently, then raised her eyes to his enquiring gaze. 'Yes, Mr Hansen', she said slowly. 'I am the girl in the picture, but perhaps now I might ask you a question?'

'Please do', he replied hastily. 1t was this moment he had thought about so often in the past, never finding a suitable reply to the question he was now required to answer.

'How did you get this photograph?' she asked directly.

Slowly and carefully, he explained the circumstances regarding his possession of the picture and of his long-held intention of finding the family of the dead soldier to try in some small way to assist them if it were possible. She followed his story silently, her arm about the shoulder of her daughter, as if in a protective way.

Softly, she spoke again. 'It is very kind of you to take so much trouble to right what appears to your eyes, a wrong. Very few people would have thought of doing what you have done for it was the War, after all, and you had to fight and our people had to do the same.'

'Yes, I suppose so', he conceded, and added flatly, 'I wasn't a particularly efficient soldier, possibly just as well in the long run.'

He felt suddenly weary and she came to him and placed a hand lightly on his shoulders.

'Stay there, Mr Hansen,' she said quietly, almost reprovingly. 'It is very remiss of me, I shall make some coffee and then we can talk some more.'

Her daughter, following her mother from the room, shyly gave him a smile of encouragement as she left. He sat still taking in his surroundings. The furniture, mainly of wood was old-looking and highly polished, and the floor carpet, although worn, was clean and brightly patterned.

Several photographs and pictures were on the walls. 1t was a tranquil house, reflecting the apparent closeness of mother and daughter, both of whom, as if echoing his thoughts, re-entered the room. They bore, between them, trays heaped with cups and saucers, milk jug, sugar bowl and a plate of small cakes. They smiled as they set out the meal on a small table, and beckoned him to join them.

The question uppermost in his mind was answered when next she spoke.

'I expect you are wondering who the people were with me in the photograph?'

He admitted quickly that this was so.

'They were my uncle - my father's brother - and his wife. They took care of me after my father was killed and my mother went into hospital shortly after his death. Both were very good to me and I remember so well how unhappy I was when I heard he had been killed in Africa.'

She seemed to sense that her remark, innocently frank in intention, distressed him, and looked at him intensely as if to convey that it was needless to castigate himself for an act committed so long ago.

He knew that she, too, had known much of loss and unhappiness, yet was not embittered and was so obviously trying to alleviate his feelings of guilt. Life could not have been all that easy for them, and tentative arrangements to help them suggested themselves to him with her next question to him.

'And now that you have found us, Mr Hansen, will you be returning to your country, or will you stay here on holiday?' she enquired easily.

He had given little actual thought to his future intentions, beyond making financial provision for them, so he replied truthfully. 'I had not really decided what I was going to do, Mrs Meyer. I suppose I had intended to return to the local hotel where I have accommodation booked, and, after that, an eventual flight back home.'

Her daughter interposed excitingly, 'Couldn't Mr Hansen stay with us mummy, and not go back to his hotel?'

Her mother, obviously not expecting her daughter's interjection, quickly supported her however. 'You are more than welcome to stay with us. We have a spare bedroom in which we have accommodated guests on holiday here. Mostly bed and breakfast stays, as I have a part-time job in the village and I am away from morning until early afternoon nearly every weekday. So, if you stayed, it would be a case of fending for yourself during my absence. Most of our other guests have gone touring or on day trips during their stay, so we have usually coped quite well.'

'And you daughter?' he asked solicitously. 'How does she manage?'

'Oh, Kathi comes with me in the morning, and I take her to school. She is usually home by 4pm each afternoon, so we do have a successful family life in spite of everything.'

'In that case, I shall be most happy to accept your kind offer and would, of course, meet your usual terms.'

She smiled. 'That would depend on the length of your stay with us.'

'Well, say three weeks, if that would not inconvenience you?'

'Oh no,' she replied quickly. 'That would be fine, and at weekends we could show you some of our beautiful countryside.' She hesitated -'that is, of course, if you would like that?'

'I'd like nothing better, Mrs Meyer.'

'Please call me Karen, Mr Hansen, after all, we are now friends, aren't we, so perhaps we may call you Martin?'

'Please do, and I shall try to be a model guest.'

'We think you are already, don't we Kathi?' She turned to her daughter who gave her a hug of affirmation.

After explaining that he would attend to his affairs in the village, he left, promising to return the following evening. Early next day, he arranged with his bank by letter and with a local solicitor who found time in a busy day to attend to his request, to make an annuity of a reasonable sum to be paid monthly to her daughter. To be held in Trust if necessary, until her majority was reached.

That evening, he was taken to his room in the cottage. Small, but extremely comfortable, its wardrobe was ample for his few clothes. Gaily coloured curtains draped the window overlooking the rear garden, and the last rays of sunshine lanced through the window and bronzed all they touched. Utterly content, he turned to see Karen looking at him.

'You are happy here, aren't you?'

A reply was unnecessary and he merely smiled and nodded in agreement.

The next two weeks passed most pleasantly for, having extended the hire period of the car, he was able to take mother and daughter to the various places of interest and especial beauty spots they wanted him to see and share with them. They returned to the cottage each evening happy in each other's company, recounting the events of their day.

One evening, when in his room, Karen knocked and asked to enter. He was brushing his hair and in the dressing table mirror, he saw her smiling reflection as she came into the room and sought out his eyes with hers. She wore a simple white blouse, a skirt and a blue stone at her throat. Approaching him, she removed the brush from his hands and placed it on the dressing table. She held his hands within her own soft, cool ones. As if by instinct, he raised her slender pointed fingers and kissed them lightly. As he did so, he pressed himself close to her. A mutual need of affection seemed to underlie their actions as he felt her body arch within his embrace.

'Thank you for being here with us, Martin,' she said warmly. 'Kathi has been especially pleased because of your many kindnesses towards her. When her father died in a road accident all those years ago, she had scarcely known him, so you've become a father figure almost to her.'

They had already spoken about their mutual backgrounds to some extent, and he was aware that the insurance paid resultant upon her husband's death had enabled the purchase of the cottage and a certain freedom from immediate financial problems. 1t was the fact that she was so lovely a person in all respects, kind almost beyond belief, and yet very much alone, that had caused him somewhat awkwardly, to ask her if she had ever considered remarrying. Her reply was that she would have liked to have done so if only for the sake of her daughter, but did not expect to find a person prepared to take on a ready-made family.

He had quietly conceded that possibility. 'There had been a few in whom I became interested, but they were not particularly keen on marriage. So,' she had sighed, 'the years just went by and I became older and less of an attraction, I suppose.'

He still recalled his instant reply, 'Never, to me, Karen', and her shy acceptance of his unselfconscious compliment. 1t seemed as if from that point onwards, they willingly allowed their closeness to develop in it own almost predetermined way. And now, at this moment, in the comfort of their embrace, he felt a surge of desire that he had once been willing to forget. He was not sure whether he should go further, and felt a slight relief when she drew slowly away from his arms and left the room.

He stood by the open window when she had gone, and felt again within him, the soft warmth of her body. He, too, had been alone for many years since his young wife had died shortly after their marriage at the end of the War. 'Acute Myeloid Leukaemia,' the death certificate had baldly stated, and it seemed then so unfair, particularly since he had lost his entire family during a heavy bombing raid. Over the years, he had wondered why such things had to be and experience had slowly taught him that life had to go on and he lived according to its own fateful rules. No-one appeared to miss out in any special way. All had their trials and tribulations and high spots of happiness to make up a kind of balance sheet. But he did admit that he did so miss the supreme happiness of the short time spent with his wife. With Karen and her daughter, he had found it was possible to let long lost feelings once again emerge. Love and affection had every right to manifest themselves - they appeared to be the ultimate gifts freely given to those in need.

Kathi had already broken up from her school for the summer holidays, and it was arranged that same evening that within the final week of his stay, they would visit a nearby lake and, since the weather was fine, perhaps swim there. He didn't have a costume, he said, but was prepared to watch, sunbathe and be utterly content to do so. These days spent with them had revealed to him the barrenness of his life during the preceding years. He supposed that he possessed basically a friendly nature, but had lacked a reason for making an effort to slough off the strongly held mistrust in his capabilities. Set in his ways, loathe to bring about a radical change, he had let his conscientious attention to his work as a minor civil servant become a form of refuge. Clerical trivia demanded little true initiative or responsibility.

That night he lay awake as his mind ranged over the events of the day, especially Karen's demonstration of affection earlier. He knew he had longed for the closeness they had briefly shared, and yet had not wanted to initiate anything of a nature likely to mar their companionship. He lay, wide-eyed, partially dreaming of the days yet to pass before his eventual return to his home country.

He sensed, rather than heard, Karen quietly enter the room and close the door behind her. A blue dressing gown covered her long white nightdress, her bare small feet silent upon the carpet. 'I couldn't sleep, either, Martin,' she said shyly, by way of explanation for her presence.

Emotionally aware of her warmth and tenderness, with his arm he made a cavern of the bedclothes and drew her close to him. All tension and shyness between them vanished as her soft lips met his own. An unspoken need, urgent and brooking no denial overwhelmed them. Days and nights of loneliness vanished as their hands ran over each other seeking that in the other they did not in themselves possess. A warm glow suffused them as they lay still and silent listening to each other's swollen breaths. He smiled at her as she lay within his arms and her physical reply compelled again a fusing of their bodies. He felt as though he had been enclosed between the folded wings of a beautiful butterfly as he slipped away into the quiet depths of a dreamless sleep. When he awoke, he was alone and he lay for a while uncertain as to whether or not it had been real. But his body provided him with the reality of the night. 1t was not a dream and it would always remain that way. An intense feeling of gratitude, affection, love, need, desire, excitement - all these feelings mingled inside him and he knew that simply basking in them would not bring her return.

He was not quite certain how to meet her gaze at breakfast. She had a warm, knowing look and bestowed a smile upon everything she looked at or touched. Their faces lit up automatically whenever their eyes met. Even Kathi, he thought, must be aware of his love for her mother. He was so blatant in expressing it. All he knew for a fact was that he did not intend to leave their lives - they were a necessary part of him and seemed to have been so since time was but a word. Later, as he drove them to the selected lake, the car packed with all the requirements, including a picnic basket, he thought long and hard as to ways and means he could remain with them.

There were many possibilities, and he would give attention to them all later. Meanwhile, there was the long, sunny day ahead to be enjoyed in their company.

The locality they chose was some distance from a group of summer villas built close to the edge of the lake. Both mother and daughter changed into their costumes in the car as he set out the picnic items on a rug near the water's edge. They then ran laughing to the lake. 'It looks a bit chilly to me,' he said.

'Not once you are in the water, Martin', she sang out as they slowly waded into the lake. Leisurely, they swam out into the deeper water and he heard their mutual laughter rippling across the lake's surface.

It was warm, almost close and humid, with a suspicion of rain building up in the clouds forming over the distant hills. The grass was fresh and cool to his touch, and the nearby willow trees were reflected in the shallower edge. Concentric ripples in the shaded water showed from time to time as small fish lazily broke the surface in search of insects hovering beneath the arched lower branches of the trees.

Time seemed motionless with the sun shining fiercely from the unrelieved blueness of the sky immediately above. It was the insistent barking of a dog in a party of holidaymakers nearby that brought his reverie to an end. Some 50 yards from the lake edge he saw Karen supporting her daughter. Her shout for help was simultaneous with his action in kicking off his shoes and speeding into the lake. He swam urgently towards them. There was no time for fear or further thought and the initial coolness of the water was imperceptible as he drove his arms deep into the water, furiously impelling himself forward.

On reaching them, he quickly relieved Karen of the task of supporting her daughter and, in fiercely gasped orders, told her to make for the shore alone. This she refused to do and remained treading water trying to assist him. Kathi, seemingly, had been attacked by cramp and was panicking as he endeavoured to support her above the surface. Several times her flaying limbs struck him as he tried to turn her on her back with the intention of pulling her to the shallower water. Repeatedly, during their slow progress he took quantities of water into his lungs and noticeably felt his strength ebbing as a result of his exertions.

Aware that Karen was close at hand, he pushed Kathi towards her as he realized that his strength alone was insufficient to save the child. Suddenly, all was blueness, the sky, the lake surface, the water's depth, the very inner retina of his eyes. Then, just as quickly, the blueness changed to fragments of air and light inextricably mixed so that he knew not one from the other. Above him was life and the green loveliness of earth, but, strong as his desire was to grasp them, an engulfing blackness steadily loosened his resolve.

His outstretched fingers tore weakly at the waters which imprisoned him and their flurried surface became slowly still as Martin Hansen, former Unteroffizier, 125 Regiment, German Afrika Korps, sank forever downwards in the dark depths - his self-imposed debt repaid.

“ADESTE FIDELISN”

The Commando Memorial near Spean Bridge, at thefoot of Glen Spean, Inverness-shire

ENTRY

Ship's Log, Norwegian Fishing Vessel "KRISTIAN" 29 December, 1973, 1700 hours outward bound from BERGEN destination fishing grounds N.W. of TRONDHEIM. Drifting 17 feet LAPWING Sailing Sloop "NONA", 2.6 tons Thames Measurement, located position Lat. 62° 45' North: Long. 4° 30' East - No one aboard sloop which had storm jib and reefed mainsail set. Navigation lights on, Sail Number. 18. Clean neat interior and last recorded entry in boat's log referred to position Lat. 62° North: Long. 3° 45' East. Port of departure not shown. No indication as to identity of crew thought to be but one person. Articles found aboard include:-

> 1 Sleeping Bag; calor gas container empty; 12 volt battery 1/4 charged; 2 gallons water; depleted food stocks; eight lines of verse headed 'V' 28.12.41. attached to last entry in log book; one empty drug bottle labelled 250 mgm tabs. Morphia, Lot no MB 14756-1. Expiry date March 1974; empty half bottle of brandy and usual adjuncts, flares, grapnel anchor, warps, plastic sextant, compass etc. Boat taken in tow to FLORO at mouth of FORDEFJORD and left in keeping of Harbour Master with report on attendent circumstances of recovery.

REPORT

Acting British Consul, British Embassy, Oslo, to Foreign Office "Re details as shown above, enquiries requested regarding abandoned sloop and origin of drugs Lot number as quoted".

CORRESPONDENCE

Inspector UV to C/Supt. 'U' Division - Ref 1'046/1735/73 "Lapwing Marine Limited; records show Sail Number 18 allotted to one of first craft manufactured and purchased in January 1969 by Mr. R. Greenway, 'Top Trees', Rainham, Essex, who still owns vessel and possesses original sails with figure 18 preceded by letter 'L'. All other enquiries negative."

ENQUIRY
of British Register of Shipping "NONA" - no record for vessel of this name of the specification shown.

REGISTER CHECK
CID Essex County Police Force - Re Schedule Dangerous Drugs - Pharmaceutical Manufacturer confirms Batch 42/4 containing Lot MB 14756-1 as part of consignment despatched for distribution SE Essex area. Detailed enquiries proceeding regarding pharmacists receiving individual lots and subsequent prescription of same. Further report will follow.

VERSE
found aboard abandoned sloop "NONA"

SEA BURIAL ' V' 28.12.41
Let Death's anchor take me down
Fluked fathoms deep
Leaving the daylight trapped above
The running tides where mermaids weep

Where wavering tendrils soft entomb
Amidst the sea-green maze
Forever in the darkened womb
Skull eyed the watered gaze

EXTRACT
From official WAR HISTORY, VOL 1 .... In the gathering darkness as the Norwegian coastline receded from view a burial service was quietly read aboard the troop ship 'Prince Harold' and the bodies of three members of 18 Commando - Captain David, whose grieving troops had refused to leave him to be buried by the

Germans, and two badly wounded men who had died while undergoing treatment in the Ship's sick-bay were committed to the deep.

INQUIRY REPORT

Register Births and Deaths (Foreign Section) - Recorded Burials at sea in Norwegian territorial waters include those of:

Captain J. David, Troop Commander,	18 Commando
Sergeant T. Halloway	18 Commando
Trooper L. Bryant	18 Commando

.... on 28.12.41 following Commando raid on the off-shore islands of VIGSO and MELLOS.

FURTHER REPORT

CID Essex County Police. Drugs in question related to prescription issued to a Mr. C. Johns, by Dr. J. Willcox, MB who, on 8 October 1973, forwarded a blood specimen of his patient for Pathological tests - acute Myeloid Leukaemia diagnosed - limited life expectancy. Mr. Johns a widower, age 54, no living relatives, absent from his home since mid-November 1973. Present whereabouts unknown.

OBITUARY

Commando News Letter - Spring 1974 - Trooper Johns Charles (18 Commando) formerly batman to late Troop Commander, passed away 28.12.73. More detailed information of the above may be obtained on application to the General Secretary.

Printed in the United Kingdom
by Lightning Source UK Ltd.
116424UKS00001B/211-228